"If you don't remember anything, why did you keep asking for me?"

"Because of this." She moved her hand to the front of her shirt. Then stopped. "I need to show you something, and I don't want you to shoot me."

"Is it another gun or knife?" he growled.

"No. It's a message."

Everything inside Jameson went still. "What kind of message?"

Her hands were shaking when she unbuttoned her blood-soaked top. Some of the blood had gone through to her chest, too, and that was why it took Jameson a moment to see the small piece of paper that she took from her bra. She unfolded it, the trembling in her hands getting even worse, and she showed it to him.

What the heck?

"Kill Jameson Beckett or you'll never see her again."

ROUGHSHOD JUSTICE

USA TODAY Bestselling Author
DELORES FOSSEN

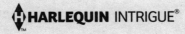

Recycling programs for this product may not exist in your area.

ISBN-13: 978-1-335-63907-3

Roughshod Justice

Copyright © 2018 by Delores Fossen

Printed in U.S.A.

Delores Fossen, a *USA TODAY* bestselling author, has sold over fifty novels, with millions of copies of her books in print worldwide. She's received a Booksellers' Best Award and an RT Reviewers' Choice Best Book Award. She was also a finalist for a prestigious RITA® Award. You can contact the author through her website at www.deloresfossen.com.

Books by Delores Fossen

Harlequin Intrigue

Blue River Ranch

Always a Lawman
Gunfire on the Ranch
Lawman from Her Past
Roughshod Justice

The Lawmen of Silver Creek Ranch

Grayson
Dade
Nate
Kade
Gage
Mason
Josh
Sawyer
Landon
Holden

HQN Books

A Wrangler's Creek Novel

Lone Star Cowboy
(ebook novella)
Those Texas Nights
One Good Cowboy
(ebook novella)
No Getting Over a Cowboy
Just Like a Cowboy
(ebook novella)
Branded as Trouble
Cowboy Dreaming
(ebook novella)
Texas-Sized Trouble

Visit the Author Profile page at Harlequin.com.

CAST OF CHARACTERS

Texas Ranger Jameson Beckett—He's out for justice. Two years ago the woman he thought he loved disappeared without a trace, but now Kelly Stockwell is back with a killer on her trail and a string of secrets that puts them both in grave danger.

Kelly Stockwell—An injury has left this PI with gaps in her memory, but she doesn't need to remember the intense attraction between Jameson and her because it's still there. Kelly's terrified, though, that the secrets locked in her mind will not only tear them apart but will also get them killed.

Mandy Stockwell—Kelly's sister. She claims she's trying to help Kelly and Jameson, but is she the one behind the attacks?

Gracelyn—A toddler who's in danger because of the attempts to kill Jameson and Kelly. But whose child is she?

Sheriff Gabriel Beckett—He's not sure what's going on between Kelly and his brother, Jameson, but he's willing to put his own life on the line to make sure the killer doesn't get to them.

August Canton—This cattleman has a long-standing feud with the Becketts because Gabriel and Jameson helped convict August's brother of murder. Maybe August is willing to kill to settle an old score.

Agent Lawrence Boyer—He's a deep-cover operative in the justice department, and he claims Gracelyn is his kidnapped daughter. But Boyer could be lying, and worse, he could be using the child to stop Jameson from finding out that he's an agent on the take.

Chapter One

Texas Ranger Jameson Beckett felt his stomach twist into a hard knot. There was too much blood on the ground. Of course, a single drop was too much, but there was enough for there to be multiple dead bodies.

What the devil had happened here?

He stepped around the first pool of blood, around the CSI who was photographing it. There were cops. Medics. The medical examiner. Chaos. A flurry of adrenaline-laced movement, something that came with the territory of a crime scene like this.

The sun was already setting, but Jameson picked through the dusky light and the chaos, looking for his brother, Gabriel, who was the sheriff. Gabriel wasn't the biggest guy in the mix, but he had an air of authority that made him easy to spot. Jameson made his way to him.

"How bad is it?" Jameson asked.

Of course, he partly knew the answer to that. It had to be bad for his brother to call in the Rangers to assist. Gabriel only did that when it was too much for him and his deputies to handle. Those were situations that didn't happen very often in Blue River, the small ranching community they called home.

"We've got two dead bodies." Gabriel tipped his head to the pair just a few yards away.

They were both men, both sprawled out in the pasture as if they'd collapsed in those spots. There was a black SUV not far from them on the road, the doors open, the engine still running.

Since the blood was between the SUV and the men, they'd likely been shot in or near the vehicle and then had gone into the pasture. Maybe to escape their attacker or maybe in pursuit of the person who'd shot them. Then the men had either succumbed to their injuries or been shot again.

Jameson turned back to his brother. "Any idea what we're dealing with? A drug deal gone bad, maybe?"

"No drugs that we can find. But both men were heavily armed. So was she." Gabriel motioned toward the ambulance that was parked just behind his cruiser.

"She?" Jameson asked.

Since it was a simple question, Jameson was more than a little surprised that his brother didn't jump to answer. Instead, Gabriel started leading him in that direction. "I don't know who she is, she won't say, but she keeps asking for you. That's why I called you."

Hell. This could be connected to one of his investigations. He had a couple of female criminal informants helping him with a homicide, and Jameson hoped one of them hadn't been involved in this.

Gabriel stopped to talk to one of the CSIs, and Jameson went ahead to the back of the ambulance, where he immediately saw someone else he knew. Cameron Doran, a deputy in the Blue River sheriff's office. Cameron was also about to be Jameson's brother-in-law since he was engaged to Jameson's kid sister Lauren. Cameron had his hand on his holstered weapon, and he was clearly standing guard.

"Has the woman told you who she is or what happened?" Jameson wanted to know.

"No. She hasn't given us much of anything. She just keeps repeating your name."

Jameson braced himself for the worst, because if his CI was in an ambulance, then she'd clearly been hurt.

And she had been.

The first thing he saw was more blood. It

was on her clothes, in her pale blond hair and all over her face, making it hard for him to tell who the heck she was.

"It's not as bad as it looks," one of the medics volunteered. According to his name tag, he was Chip Reynolds. "Head wounds just bleed a lot. It appears she got clubbed, so she needs stitches. She also probably has a concussion, but the doc will need to confirm that. Can we go ahead and take her to the hospital?"

"Not just yet." Jameson wanted to know who and what he was dealing with, and he figured Gabriel would want to know that, as well.

Jameson moved closer, leaning down so he could make eye contact with the woman. Her head whipped up, their gazes connecting. He still didn't recognize her, but he wasn't seeing much of her, either, because of the blood.

"Who are you?" he demanded.

She opened her mouth, closed it and looked up at the EMT as if expecting him to know. He just lifted his shoulder. "She didn't have any ID on her," the medic explained.

"Are you Jameson Beckett?" she said to him.

"I asked first." But then he paused and replayed what he'd just heard.

Hell.

He didn't recognize her hair, her eyes or her

face with all that blood, but Jameson sure as heck recognized the voice.

"Kelly?"

Jameson went even closer, and the medic helped by wiping off some of the blood. Yeah, it was Kelly Stockwell all right.

"I thought you were dead," Jameson grumbled.

She blew out a breath, and it sounded like one of relief. Though Jameson couldn't figure out what she was relieved about. She was injured, and there were two dead bodies just yards away from her.

"You know me," Kelly whispered after another of those breaths.

Clearly, this was some kind of sick joke. "Of course I know you."

He had the memories to prove it, too. Memories of Kelly being in his bed. Also memories of her disappearing without so much as a text. Jameson truly hadn't thought she was dead, though, only that she'd run out after she'd gotten what she wanted from him.

And it hadn't been sex that she'd wanted.

"Your sister thinks you're dead, too," he added, just to get his mind back on the right track.

"I have a sister?"

Jameson didn't roll his eyes, but it was close. "Mandy. Ring any bells?"

"No." But she seemed to latch right onto that. "Is she okay?"

"I have no idea. Mandy and I haven't talked in months."

They had in the beginning, though, after Kelly disappeared about two years ago. Jameson had spent several months looking for her without so much as a clue to her whereabouts. Mandy had helped with that. *Some*. Not nearly enough, considering her sister was missing, but Jameson figured not all siblings were as close as he was to his brother and sisters. After that initial search for Kelly had turned up empty, he'd put both the woman and his hunt for her on the back burner.

"Can you call Mandy and make sure she's all right?" Kelly asked. Except it was more than a plea for help. It was a demand.

Jameson huffed. "I thought you said you didn't remember her."

"I don't, but…please, just call or text her."

Jameson considered refusing, but since Mandy could indeed be connected to this, and even if she wasn't, she would want to know that Kelly was alive. He scrolled through his contacts, located Mandy's number and called her. No answer, but when it went to voice mail, Jameson asked her to get in touch with him ASAP.

Kelly thanked him under her breath. Paused. "You're…angry with me," she muttered. "Why?"

A burst of air left his mouth. Definitely not a laugh from humor. "You stole a file about an investigation from my office in my house," he snapped.

Yes, it seemed a bad time to bring that up, especially considering that Kelly obviously had much more serious problems on her hands, but hell in a handbasket, it stung that he'd been so wrong about her. Jameson had trusted her, and she'd pretended to like him so she could get her hands on the file.

The file itself wasn't one of Jameson's cases. Not officially anyway. But it had been a compilation of everything that had to do with his parents' murders. It had statements of witnesses' accounts, court records and even notes from the investigations his father was working on when he'd been murdered.

She shook her head. "I don't remember anything."

"That's convenient." Jameson didn't bother taking out the sarcasm. "We'll get to that stolen file later. Right now, tell me about those dead men."

Kelly closed her eyes for a moment. Gave a

heavy sigh. "Several people have already asked me that. I don't know what happened. I don't know who they are. I don't know who I am."

He didn't repeat the "convenient" comment, but that's exactly what Jameson was thinking.

Of course, it was possible she did have some memory loss. That was a nasty gash near her hairline, and the medic had said she might have a concussion. But pretending to have amnesia would be a quick way for Kelly not to have to answer any of his questions.

Jameson didn't get a chance to say anything else to her. That's because Gabriel finished his chat with the CSI and joined them.

"So who is she?" Gabriel immediately asked Jameson.

"Kelly Stockwell."

She repeated that as if trying to figure out if it was right or if she recognized it. Either she didn't or else was faking it, and tears sprang to her eyes.

A first.

Kelly wasn't the crying sort.

"She's not linked to the…other stuff going on, is she?" Gabriel asked.

Jameson didn't need him to clarify "the other stuff." They were just two days away from the tenth anniversary of their parents' brutal murders. Murders that had been splattered over every newspaper in the state, and because of all that news coverage, it had brought out a couple of crazies. People who'd wanted to see the old crime scene. Others who'd talked of copycat killings.

At least his parents' killer, Travis Canton, was behind bars and was no longer a threat. Of course, there were some, and Kelly was one of them, who thought the wrong man had been convicted.

Jameson didn't see it that way. Travis and his father had had plenty of run-ins over the land boundaries they shared. Added to that, Travis was a drunk. A mean one. And Jameson believed it was in one of those mean rages that Travis had slipped into the Beckett home and knifed Jameson's dad. When his mother saw what was going on, Travis killed her, too.

And that was the theory the prosecution had used to give Travis a life sentence.

"She's connected in a way," Jameson verified. "She's a PI, and she and her sister, Mandy, owned an agency in San Antonio. A few years back, August hired them to find any evidence to clear Travis's name."

No need to clarify to Gabriel who August was. He was Travis's half brother and a pain because he was always pushing hard to come up with someone else who could have murdered the Becketts. That way, he could spring his brother from jail.

That wasn't going to happen.

At least not with anything August might have gotten from Kelly and Mandy. Even though there hadn't been any new evidence to find, that hadn't stopped Kelly from digging. And she'd done her digging by getting close to Jameson so she could steal that file.

"I didn't know what Kelly was up to when I met her about two years ago," Jameson went on. "I didn't know she was working for August. But when I found out, she disappeared, and her sister eventually closed the business."

Jameson didn't mention anything about his sleeping with Kelly. Didn't have to do that. Gabriel slid him a glance to let him know that he knew. It was that sixth sense that his big brother had.

"I take it there's some bad history...and more...between you two," Gabriel added, and he aimed a look at Kelly.

"You could say that. At best she's a liar and a thief. She stole everything I had about our parents' murder investigation, including files with info that hadn't been released to the public." Obviously, though, that was the least of her worries right now. "Who found her?" Jameson asked. "Who called this in?"

"A guy driving by saw the two men in the pasture, and Kelly was running away. Or rather trying to do that. She collapsed near the ditch. Since she was armed, the guy didn't get out of his truck, but he called it in. I had him go to the station to wait for me, and I'll question him later."

Good. Jameson wanted to hear what the man had to say. But more than that, he wanted to finish this conversation with Kelly.

"I can ride in the ambulance with her to the hospital," Jameson offered.

Gabriel didn't exactly jump to agree to that. Probably because he knew Jameson wasn't in the best of moods. Still, Gabriel also knew that Jameson wouldn't do anything to disrespect the badge. It didn't mean, however, that he wouldn't grill Kelly. As much as he could grill an injured woman anyway.

"Watch your step with her," Gabriel warned him as Jameson got into the ambulance. "When I frisked her, she had two guns and a knife, and she would have hit me with a karate chop if I hadn't gotten out of the way in time."

"I thought you were going to try to kill me," Kelly said.

Jameson hadn't even been sure she was listening, but she obviously was. He also hadn't remembered Kelly having any martial arts skills. Of course, probably everything she'd told him about herself was a lie. As far as Jameson was concerned, he didn't really know the woman in front of him.

"Are you going to try to kill me?" she came out and asked, glancing first at Gabriel and Cameron. Then at Jameson.

Jameson tapped his badge. "I'm not the bad guy here."

Her gaze darted away from his, and she took another of those uneasy breaths. "Sometimes bad guys wear badges."

That didn't sound like a guess or a general observation. "Is your amnesia cured and you're remembering something specific?" Jameson pressed.

But he instantly regretted the snark. More tears came, and even though Kelly quickly brushed them away—cursed them, too—Jameson still saw the pain on her face. Not just physical pain, either. Whether or not the amnesia was real, she'd still been through some kind of ordeal.

"The CSI swabbed her hands for gunshot residue," Gabriel explained, "but she put up a real fight about being fingerprinted."

Jameson pulled back his shoulders. People who did that usually didn't want their identities known. Coupled with the dyed hair—Kelly had been a brunette when he'd met her—she was obviously trying to disguise her appearance. Even her eyes were different. She'd hidden her green eyes with brown contacts.

"Call me if she says anything we can use to figure this out," Gabriel added, shutting the ambulance door.

Jameson nodded and got seated just as the ambulance driver took off. The EMT continued to hold a compress to Kelly's head and probably would have to do that the entire time since it was still bleeding.

It wouldn't be a long ride to the hospital, only about ten minutes, and Jameson wanted to make the most of that time. He started by reading Kelly her rights. Gabriel had likely already done that, but Jameson didn't want there to be any unticked boxes if she did confess to everything.

Whatever "everything" was.

"Did you shoot those two men?" he asked. "And before you lie, just remember we'll know if you've fired a gun because there'll be gunshot residue on your hands. Your weapons will be tested, too."

She touched her fingers to her mouth, which was trembling a little. "I honestly don't know if I shot them or not. They're dead?"

He nodded, though the confirmation might

not have even been necessary. Because she might already know the answer. "Who were they?"

An immediate head shake that time. So fast that the medic told her to keep still. "I don't know that, either," Kelly answered. Her gaze came to Jameson's again. "Did you send them after me?"

There it was again—her distrust of him. Well, the feeling was mutual. "Let's get something straight. I didn't send thugs after you. I'm not here to kill you. Everything I've told you has been the truth, but you can't say the same, can you?"

She stared at him. "You're talking about that file you mentioned to the sheriff. I don't remember it. I need to remember," she added as she choked back a hoarse sob. "Because I have to know who you really are and why this is happening."

He huffed again. "I'm really Jameson Beckett, Texas Ranger," he supplied. "Now, start from the beginning. Tell me everything you know, everything you remember."

"I remember them," she said, glancing at Chip and the other EMTs. "And the sheriff. Someone swabbed my hands."

That was a good start, but nowhere near what he wanted. "What do you recall before that?"

Jameson pressed. "Before the sheriff and the EMTs arrived."

Kelly stayed quiet for several moments. "I remember the pain in my head. Being on the ground. It was damp. And I saw the blood." She stopped, her gaze going to his again. "What did the sheriff mean when he said there's a bad history *and more* between us?"

Well, there was nothing wrong with her short-term memory, that was for certain. Jameson didn't answer her, but he thought she understood what he wasn't saying because she muttered a simple response.

"Oh." Then she groaned. "Oh, God." The tears filled her eyes again. "But it doesn't make sense."

"I agree. Not much about this makes sense, but you mean something specific. What exactly?" When she didn't answer, Jameson added another question, one that was at the top of his list of things he wanted to know. "If you don't remember anything, why did you keep asking for me?"

"Because of this." She moved her hand to the front of her shirt. Then stopped. "I need to show you something, and I don't want you to shoot me."

"Is it another gun or knife?" he growled. Because he was pretty sure his brother would have found something like that when he frisked her.

"No. It's a message."

Everything inside Jameson went still. "What kind of message?"

Her hands were shaking when she unbuttoned her top. Some of the blood had soaked through to her chest, too, and that's why it took Jameson a moment to see the small piece of paper that she took from her bra. She unfolded it, the trembling in her hands getting even worse, and she showed it to him.

What the heck?

Jameson drew his gun. "Explain that," he demanded, tipping his head to the note.

Or rather the threat.

Kill Jameson Beckett or you'll never see her again.

Chapter Two

Kelly hadn't been sure what Jameson's reaction would be, but she'd known it wouldn't be good. And it wasn't.

The anger flared through those already-intense blue eyes.

Eyes that she wished she could remember.

There was something about him that tugged at her. Attraction, probably. He was a hot cowboy after all. But there seemed to be something else. Something that she wished would become clearer in her muddled mind. Clearer because the last thing she wanted to do was kill this man.

He was glaring at her now, but still she studied him. Hoping there was something about him that would trigger a memory. He was tall and lanky. Dark brown hair like his brother. The family resemblance was there as well, but it wasn't a resemblance that caused her to recall anything other than what'd happened to her in the past half hour or so.

"Who wrote that message?" Jameson snarled. He snapped a picture of it with his phone and sent the photo to someone. Probably the sheriff. Then, taking the note just by the edge, he snatched it from her and put it on the seat next to him.

Kelly buttoned up her top. She definitely didn't want to sit there with her bra exposed. "I don't know who wrote it or how I got it."

That was the truth. And it was something she figured she'd be saying a lot tonight. She prayed this memory loss was temporary. Prayed, too, that her injuries weren't so serious that she couldn't get the heck out of there ASAP. Other than the attraction she was feeling toward Jameson, she knew in her gut that it wasn't safe to be here.

Plus, there was the "her" in the message.

It was obvious someone—a woman—was in danger.

"I think it could mean my sister," she added. "That's why I had you try to call her. Could you try again, please?"

He glared at her, hesitated, but he did fire off a text to someone. Kelly had no memories of Mandy, but if those dead men had taken her, their comrades could be holding her somewhere.

Waiting for Kelly to do what they'd demanded and kill Jameson.

"If you really have amnesia," Jameson went on, still snarling, "how did you know that message was there?"

"I just knew." It was an answer that obviously didn't please him, because he cursed. "Why would someone want you dead?" she asked.

Jameson gave her another of those flat, scowled looks. "I'm a Texas Ranger, and I've put a lot of people in jail. One of them might not be happy about that."

Yes, it could be that. But she had the feeling there was more to it. Jameson confirmed that several seconds later.

"My family has been getting threatening emails and letters." His jaw clenched. "Threats connected to my parents, who were murdered ten years ago. The killer is in a maximum security prison, but someone has been sending out these sick messages to taunt us." He tipped his head to the note. "Messages like that one."

"Is there a *her* in any of those emails or letters?" she asked.

"No. But that doesn't mean it's not from the same person. Are you the one threatening us, Kelly?"

She tried to pick through the tornado in her head but couldn't latch onto anything. Other than the pain. "I don't think so. No," she amended. She didn't want to harm Jameson. Didn't want to harm anyone. She just wanted to figure out what the heck was going on. "Was I connected to your parents' murders, to their killer?"

Now it was his turn to shake his head. "Not to the murders but to August Canton. His brother is the one who was convicted of killing my folks. August somehow convinced you of his brother's innocence, so you were looking for anything to help with the appeals. You stole from me to do that."

Yes, she'd heard the conversation that he'd had with his brother about the stolen file. Again, no memory, and it didn't seem like something she would have done. Especially steal from a man who'd likely been her lover.

Kelly repeated August Canton's name, hoping it would trigger something. It didn't. "I don't remember him, either. Could any of this be linked to August or his brother?"

"Not Travis, because he's in jail." Then he paused. "But even if August or he managed to arrange something like this, I can't imagine either of them going about it this way. You're not a hired gun. Or at least you weren't two years ago."

And she wasn't now. Kelly was certain of

that. However, she didn't get a chance to try to convince him because the ambulance pulled to a stop in front of the emergency room doors of the hospital. The EMTs used the gurney to take her inside.

There was a uniformed deputy waiting for them, and when they went in, Jameson immediately motioned toward the note that he'd left on the seat. "Bag that and show it to Gabriel. I'll need her clothes bagged, too."

Yes, because there might be some kind of evidence on them. She hoped so anyway. She needed answers.

"Who were those dead men in the pasture?" she asked. "Do you have ID's on them?"

Jameson seemed annoyed with her question. Of course, he probably was annoyed—and highly concerned—about all of this. Because of the note that had ordered her to kill him.

"We'll know more soon," he finally answered. "Especially when you remember what you should be remembering."

There it was again, the tone that indicated he didn't believe her. She couldn't blame him. There were two dead guys, a threatening note and an ex-lover who didn't have a clue what was going on.

The medics transferred her to an examining table in a room just off the ER, and Kelly im-

mediately looked around to make sure someone wasn't there, ready to come after her. Every
nerve in her body was on high alert, and she
prayed if there was another attack, she could
protect herself.

Jameson didn't immediately come into the
room with her, but he stayed in the doorway
while he made a call. However, he didn't take
his attention off her. Too bad. Because Kelly
thought it might be a good idea for her to put
some distance between Jameson and her.

While he was still on the phone, a nurse
came in, took her vitals and made a quick check
of her head wound. It was throbbing, but that
was the least of her problems right now. Apparently the least of Jameson's, too, because
whatever he was hearing on the phone caused
his forehead to bunch up.

"What's wrong?" she asked the moment he
ended the call.

The nurse mumbled something about the
doctor seeing her soon and walked out, leaving them alone.

"Your sister's still not answering her phone,
so I'm having the San Antonio cops go out and
check on her," Jameson said.

"Good. Thank you." But that wasn't an explanation for the renewed tension in his face.
"What else?"

"You have gunshot residue on your hands, and one of the guns you had matches the wounds on the dead guys. It's looking as if you're the one who killed them."

Kelly felt the tears again. Felt the icy slam of fear in her chest. "I don't think I had a choice. I think they were trying to kill me."

Jameson blew out a long breath. It sounded bad. *Was* bad, she mentally corrected. She'd been sent to kill him. Maybe those men had been sent to kill her. And whoever had orchestrated it was maybe still out there. Maybe that someone was also the reason her sister wasn't able to answer her phone.

Kelly tried to focus, tried to make sense of the whirl of memories that were in her throbbing head. But when she wasn't able to sort through it, she decided it was time to get as much info from Jameson as he would give her. Maybe then she could use that to piece together this puzzle.

"We were lovers?" she asked.

"No. Yes," he amended after he cursed. "We had sex, but it was all a ploy on your part to steal that file."

That. They kept going back to that file. "Why would I help someone like August Canton?"

"You tell me. In fact, I wanted to ask you

"I'm a Justice Department agent," Worley added, his attention sliding from Jameson to her. "My real name is Lawrence Boyer. And I'm here to arrest Kelly for murder."

Chapter Three

Jameson didn't know who was more stunned with Worley's announcement—him or Kelly. But Kelly did look as if she was about to try to sprint out of there. Jameson wouldn't let her do that. Nor would he take anything Worley said, or what he was wearing, at face value.

Including that badge or his name.

"Federal agent, huh?" Jameson asked him, and he didn't bother to sound even marginally convinced.

Worley blew out a long breath as if annoyed with this. Well, Jameson was annoyed, too. He didn't have time for this clown, especially since Worley could be behind the attack and Mandy's disappearance. Jameson didn't want to examine why he was suddenly on Kelly's side. But when it came to Worley, he was.

"I figured you wouldn't believe me." Worley checked his watch. "But you should be getting a call any second now from someone you will believe. Your brother, the sheriff. He's verifying now that I'm an agent. Once that's done, you'll turn Kelly over to me."

"I won't go with him," Kelly said just as Jameson snarled, "Like hell I'll turn her over to you."

That caused Kelly to look at him, and he saw not tears this time but an unspoken thanks. But a thanks wasn't going to help right now. He needed some things cleared up.

"Who are you claiming Kelly murdered?" Jameson asked.

"Those two men your brother and his deputies are investigating."

Jameson certainly couldn't deny that she had been the one to shoot them. In fact, the evidence pointed to her doing it. But the evidence was equally clear that she'd also been attacked, probably by those two men. Unless...

He didn't like even thinking it, but Jameson had to at least consider it. Kelly could be playing him again. She might have had a beef with those guys. Could have even written the note herself. But none of that felt right, especially now that Mandy was missing.

"Who were those men?" Kelly asked Worley.

Worley just stared at her. "You tell me."

"She can't," Jameson volunteered. "See that

cut on her head? Someone clubbed her, and she has amnesia."

Worley looked as skeptical about that as Jameson probably had when he'd first heard Kelly say that she couldn't remember. But some of that skepticism was fading. Worse, he suddenly felt the need to protect Kelly. Coupled with the remnants of the old attraction, that wasn't a good combination.

Jameson's phone rang, the sound slicing through the room. Slicing through him, too, because he saw Gabriel's name on the screen.

"Worley's here," Jameson answered, and he put the call on speaker so that Kelly could hear.

"Yeah. And if he told you he's a Justice Department agent, he is," Gabriel said. "I just confirmed it. His real name is Lawrence Boyer."

Kelly hadn't had much color in her face, but that rid her of what she did have. "Impossible."

Normally, Jameson would have agreed with her, but he didn't doubt anything Gabriel told him.

"My source in the Justice Department is reliable," Gabriel continued, "and according to him, Boyer aka Worley is a joe, someone who spends months or even years in deep cover."

So Boyer had told the truth, about being an agent anyway. "Does he have a court order for Kelly's arrest?" Jameson asked.

"No. Why? Is that why Boyer says he's there? Because my source couldn't tell me."

"Yep, but without a court order, Boyer's not taking our witness to what could be a double homicide. You agree?"

"Agreed," Gabriel quickly said. "You need backup?"

"Not yet. I'll call you if I do." Jameson finished the call, slipped his phone back in his pocket and turned to Agent Boyer. "Tell me everything you know about those men," Jameson demanded. "In fact, tell me everything you know about Kelly."

Boyer volleyed several glances at Kelly and him. For a moment Jameson thought he was going to have to remind this agent that the Rangers and the sheriff had jurisdiction here and that meant Boyer had to cooperate. Even if it was obvious that was the last thing he wanted to do.

"You really don't remember anything?" Boyer pressed when his attention finally settled on Kelly.

"I remember a few things." It sounded as if Kelly was carefully choosing her words. And lying. But maybe she didn't want this guy to know that she had no memory of her association with him. Perhaps it was her way of forcing Boyer to tell the truth.

"I met you and your sister about two years ago," Boyer finally started. "By then, I'd been on a deep cover assignment for well over a year, and I was posing as a money launderer so I could gather info on a cartel operating in the state. I didn't tell many people who I really was, but I told you, and I gained your trust."

"What?" Kelly snapped. She looked over the man from head to toe, and there wasn't a drop of trust in her eyes or expression.

Boyer nodded. "Mandy and you were working for my ex, Hadley." His mouth tightened when he said her name. "She was accusing me of stealing our newborn daughter, but you soon realized she was just doing that to get back at me because I'd broken things off with her. After that, you agreed to help me."

Jameson went through that info, but it only created more questions. "Hadley knew you were an agent?"

"No. And that should tell you something about her. She got involved with me while thinking I was a criminal."

Jameson lifted his shoulder. "It tells me something about you, too. It tells me you were lying to a woman pregnant with your child."

Boyer's mouth tightened even more, and his eyes were narrowed when he turned to Jameson. "The pregnancy was an accident. On my part anyway. I think Hadley planned it to trap me into marriage. When I didn't go for that and broke off the relationship, she retaliated by accusing me of kidnapping the child just days after she was born."

As much as Jameson hated to admit it, that could all be true. He didn't know Hadley, and in his line of work, he ran into plenty of people who didn't mind bedding down with criminals.

"So what happened to your daughter?" Jameson asked.

"I don't know." Boyer scrubbed his hand over his face. "I suspect Hadley had Amy hidden away from me and the cops, and when she was killed in the car accident, the location of that hidden place died with her. Don't get me wrong. I haven't given up finding my daughter, but at the moment I've run out of leads."

Kelly made a sound, sort of a muffled moan. Maybe because she realized this could turn out to be a similar situation for her sister. With a similar ending of them never finding her. But Jameson wanted to prevent that from happening, and maybe Boyer could help with that. He was about to ask Boyer to spill all about the two dead guys, but Kelly spoke to Boyer before he could do that.

"You said you got me to trust you. How exactly did you manage that?" Kelly asked. "Because I'm certainly not feeling any trust for you now."

Boyer made a sound of agreement. "Ditto. I don't trust you, either. But your misplaced mistrust is probably because you betrayed me. That's how you got into this mess you're in right now."

Jameson moved to Kelly's side so he could face Boyer. "Explain that," Jameson insisted.

"After I told Mandy and you I was an agent, you both said you'd back off so that my cover wouldn't be blown. A blown cover could have gotten me killed by the men I was doing business with. You also agreed to help me with my assignment." Boyer paused, gathered his breath. "I needed you to get a file from Jameson."

Jameson had anticipated what Boyer might say, but he certainly hadn't anticipated *that*. He looked at Kelly to see if she was remembering any of this, but she only shook her head.

"What file?" Jameson snapped. "And why the hell not just come to me for it?"

"I didn't go to you because I didn't want you to know I was an agent. I didn't want it leaked, and at the time there were rumors that there was a mole in the Rangers."

"There wasn't a mole," Jameson argued once

he got his jaw unclenched. If so, he would have darn sure heard about it.

"I couldn't risk it. I'd already told Mandy and Kelly, but I only did that so I could get any information you had on your parents' murders."

Of course, he'd known the file that Kelly had stolen was about the murders, but he didn't care for a deep cover agent having an interest in the case. He made another circling motion for Boyer to continue.

But Boyer only said two words. "August Canton."

Now Jameson had to take a moment because the memories came. Of his parents' murders. Of the pain and grief over losing them.

"August was originally a murder suspect," Jameson said. "Several people were. But my father was also investigating a situation where a local widow, Hattie Osmond, had been milked out of lots of money. August was a suspect in that crime, too, but Hattie refused to name him. She passed away last year so there's no way to press her for the truth."

Boyer nodded. "I interviewed her. So did Kelly."

"Kelly?" Jameson repeated. She seemed just as surprised about that as he was.

"Yeah. She talked to Hattie about two years ago. And she questioned Marilyn Deavers, the woman who'd given August an alibi for the night of your parents' murders."

Jameson looked at Kelly, but she only shook her head. "I don't know why I did that. Or if I learned anything."

"Marilyn is dead now, too," Boyer went on. "She died in a car accident."

So if Marilyn had altered her story about August being with her, then there'd be no way to confirm it. Unless they found that file.

"I believe August did scam money from Hattie," Boyer continued a moment later. "Maybe others, as well. But that's not why I was investigating him. I believe August is involved in a money laundering scheme. I'd hoped there'd be something in your files that would help, something that hadn't been in any of the police and FBI reports. But there wasn't."

Kelly whispered a single word of profanity under her breath. "So I stole that file for nothing?"

"I obviously didn't know that at the time." Boyer didn't sound the least bit apologetic, either. "When I realized the file was useless, I pressed you to get more info from Jameson. You said you would, but then you disappeared."

"Why did I do that?" she asked.

"I have no idea. I didn't hear from you for two years, and then this morning, I got a fran-

Chapter Four

Kelly's breath froze. From the moment she'd been carried into the hospital, she'd had a bad feeling about this place. It just wasn't safe. And the gunman that the security guard had spotted proved it.

The gunman was after her.

She didn't need her memories to know that, but it certainly would have helped if she remembered why someone wanted her dead. Because if she knew the why, then maybe she could figure out who was behind this. And perhaps put an end to it. Of course, at the moment she wasn't in shape to stop much of anything. But she did need to get the heck out of there.

Kelly stood to do just that, but Jameson immediately made sure that didn't happen. "You're not going anywhere," he warned her. However, he did draw his gun from his holster and stepped in front of her.

Protecting her.

She figured that wasn't something he especially wanted to do, but he was a lawman, and he probably considered this to be part of his job.

"Get me some backup now and patch me through to the security guard," Jameson told Cameron. He now had the phone sandwiched between his shoulder and ear. It only took a few seconds for that to happen.

Seconds that the man in the parking lot could be using to make his way to the hospital. Kelly looked around for something, anything, she could use as a weapon, but other than some medical equipment, there wasn't much. Plus, she definitely wouldn't win a hand-to-hand fight with this guy. Not with the way her head was still spinning. She could barely stand up.

"Hank, do you still have eyes on the guy with the gun?" Jameson asked the security guard.

Jameson didn't put the call on speaker, but since Kelly was right behind him, she heard the guard answer. "Yeah, but he's on the move. He's darting from one car to another, using them for cover, but he's definitely heading this way."

Jameson growled out some profanity under his breath. "Some deputies are on the way, but if you have to, shoot this idiot. Don't go for a kill shot, though, because I'd like to take him alive." He paused. "Did another man just leave the building? Bulky build and bald?"

"No. Haven't seen anybody like that. Why? Is he dangerous, too?"

"Maybe," Jameson answered. "Just watch your back around him if he shows up. And lock down the hospital. There could be other gunmen at the front or sides of the building."

She hadn't needed anything else to rev up her heartbeat, but that did it. There could be any number of hired guns, and Kelly doubted that just locking up would keep them all out.

Jameson ended the call, putting the phone back in his pocket, and he looked at her. "I need to go to the guard to make sure this gunman doesn't get out of the parking lot. I know the guard—Hank Winston—but I have no idea if he's a good enough shot to stop this person."

And even if he was a good shot, it was too big of a risk to take. The gunman could shoot an innocent bystander. Heck, if he got inside, he could shoot Hank as well before coming after her.

"I want to go, too," Kelly insisted. "Just give me a gun."

Jameson gave her a flat look. "No gun. But I don't think it's a good idea to leave you here alone since we don't know where Boyer is. That means I want you to come with me, but I don't want you to do anything stupid."

She nearly asked Jameson what he would

consider stupid, but he didn't give her a chance to say anything. He got them moving out the door of the examining room. Fast. Too fast for Kelly to keep up with her wobbly legs, and Jameson cursed again when he glanced back at her. He looped his arm around her waist and started walking, slower this time.

"Once I take care of this," Jameson said, "you can finish up with the doctor and then I can get you to the sheriff's office. If you need protective custody, we can work it out there."

Kelly didn't miss the "if." He still didn't trust her—which was reasonable—since she couldn't remember what she'd done or why she was carrying that note ordering her to kill him.

"We need to find my sister, too," she reminded him, though Kelly was certain he remembered.

"Gabriel's looking," he assured her.

Yes, but that didn't mean she couldn't look, as well. And she would. But first she had to take care of a possible killer and then find a way to escape. Or at least find a way to get Jameson to believe her so he would help her.

No easy feat.

Apparently, they'd been lovers, but judging from the way Jameson glared at her nearly every time their eyes met, he didn't feel even a trace of affection for her. However, the attraction was still there, and perhaps that was one of the reasons he was glaring. He didn't need this heat between them any more than Kelly did.

They made their way down a wide corridor with shiny gray tile floors, and Jameson slowed when they neared the back exit. The guard was there, his gun drawn and pointed at the glass door.

"He's still out there," Hank said, sparing Jameson and her a glance. "What should I do?"

"Come over here and wait with her." Jameson tipped his head to the hall. He took up position by the side of the door so he could peer out into the parking lot. "But keep watch. I don't want anyone sneaking up on us."

Neither did Kelly, so she kept watch, as well. "Maybe if I could get a look at the gunman, I might recognize him?" she said.

Jameson spared her a glance. "Your memory's starting to come back?" There it was again. The skepticism that she'd never lost it in the first place.

"No. But seeing him might trigger something."

"Seeing him might get you killed," Jameson pointed out. "This glass is reinforced, but it's not bullet-resistant."

Which meant Jameson could be shot, too. Kelly had already put him in enough danger, so she leaned out, trying to get a glimpse of the gunman.

And she got it all right.

The tall lanky man ran from the back of an SUV to a truck. But the new position didn't put him closer to the building. Nor did his next move when he darted behind a car. He was moving laterally. Maybe so he could have a better shot?

Or was this about something else?

"Hell," Jameson said. "I think this clown is just a decoy." Obviously, he'd reached the same conclusion Kelly just had. "A second gunman's probably already in the building."

Both Hank and Kelly shot glances around them. The hall wasn't empty. There were two people wearing green scrubs, a man holding the hand of a toddler and a woman carrying a vase of flowers. All seemed to be doing normal things that people would do in a hospital.

Seemed.

The flower-carrying woman was walking slow, staying behind the man and the little boy, but Kelly didn't think they were together. She got confirmation of that when the boy stumbled and the woman didn't even reach out to break his fall. It was the man who picked up the child. He kissed the boy on the cheek and started walking again, coming up the hall toward them.

Jameson took out his phone and texted someone. Gabriel, probably. To let his brother know what was going on.

"See anyone suspicious?" Jameson asked Hank and her when he'd finished.

Hank shook his head. Kelly didn't. "The woman with the flowers could be carrying a gun," she said.

Though it wasn't visible. Still, she was wearing jeans and could have a concealed weapon in a slide holster. Plus, there was something about the intense look on her face that set off alarms inside her. So intense that Kelly moved out of her line of sight and pulled Hank next to her.

Jameson hurried from the back door just long enough to glance down the hall, and he made a frustrated sound of agreement. "We can't risk her firing shots. Not with that kid and the other innocent people standing around."

Kelly could see and feel the debate going on inside Jameson. They didn't have time to wait for backup. Nor did they have a lot of options here. If whoever was behind this had indeed set up a decoy, then there could be more than one hired killer in the hospital.

"Come on," Jameson finally said. He motioned for them to follow him to the door, and he made brief eye contact with Hank. "Keep hold of Kelly, and when we get outside, get her down behind the first vehicle you reach."

The blood rushed to her head, and Kelly felt the kick of adrenaline. And fear. So many things could go wrong right now, and staying put could be the biggest mistake of all. Still, she hated to go out there without any way to defend herself.

Hank put his arm around Kelly's waist, and the moment Jameson unlocked the door, they started moving. So did the decoy. He lifted his head, and Kelly saw the surprise register in his eyes.

It didn't last.

Because the moment the man turned his rifle in their directions, Jameson took aim and shot him square in the chest. The guy dropped like a stone, and Kelly could tell he was dead. But she could no longer see him because Hank did as Jameson said, and he pulled her to the side of a minivan.

"Do you have a backup gun or knife?" she whispered to Hank. "I'm a PI. I know how to shoot." Or at least she thought she did. Now, if she could just remember the firearms training she would have almost certainly had in order to get a private investigator's license.

Hank glanced back at her, and even though

Kelly could tell he was plenty uncertain about this, he lifted the leg of his pants and took a small handgun from his boot holster. Kelly didn't waste a second pivoting toward the door so she could keep watch for that woman who might be coming after them.

Jameson took cover as well—using the red truck on the other side of the door. And they waited.

The moments crawled by, and Kelly soon heard a welcome sound. Sirens. Backup had arrived, and maybe that meant these would-be killers would call off the attack. She wanted answers. Wanted to know who was responsible for this. But she didn't want those answers if it meant innocent people could die.

"Get down!" Jameson shouted just as a shot was fired.

Kelly expected the bullet to go in Jameson's direction. It didn't. It came in hers. The shot slammed into the minivan just inches from where Hank and she were crouching.

That sent Kelly and him scurrying to the side, but moving in any direction was a risk. Yes, Jameson had shot the decoy, but that didn't mean others weren't all over the parking lot.

But this shot had come from inside the hospital.

Kelly peered around the minivan and spotted

the woman. She was no longer carrying flowers, but she had the back door open a couple of inches. Her gun was jutting out through the space.

And she fired again.

This time at Jameson.

From their new position, Kelly could no longer see Jameson, but he'd probably tried to shoot the woman. Judging from the sounds Kelly then heard, Jameson had been forced to take cover, as well.

Kelly figured Jameson wasn't going to like what she was doing, but she leaned out enough from the minivan so she could see if she had anything close to a clean shot. She did.

And she took it.

Kelly aimed, fired, and the bullet crashed through the glass and into the woman's chest. Like her decoy comrade, she fell, but that wasn't the only sound Kelly heard. Jameson cursed—the profanity aimed at her.

"I told you to stay down," Jameson snarled, and in the same breath, there was another shot.

Sweet heaven. Who was Jameson shooting at now?

Kelly scrambled around Hank and made her way to the rear of the minivan. There, she had a good angle to see Jameson. To see the glare that he tossed her, too. Obviously, he wasn't happy that she had changed her position or that she fired that shot. Kelly wasn't especially happy about it, either, but she saw it as a necessary choice.

"Put down your gun," someone shouted.

Gabriel. He had apparently arrived with backup. Good. Kelly hoped he had brought a lot of deputies with him so they could secure the hospital.

"He's there," Hank said, motioning in the direction of the far side of the building.

There was a man carrying a handgun in the spot where Hank had indicated. However, the man didn't drop his weapon as Gabriel had ordered. He turned and fired a shot, no doubt aiming for the sheriff.

Jameson took care of the guy. He double-tapped the trigger, but he hadn't gone for kill shots. The bullets went into the man's shoulder and shooting arm. He stayed on his feet, but his gun clattered to the ground.

Suddenly, there were the sounds of footsteps. Plenty of them. And they were all converging on the injured man. With his gaze still firing all around him, Jameson reached the guy first, but Gabriel and a deputy soon joined him. Another deputy stepped out from the back door where the gunwoman was still sprawled out. She was almost certainly dead. It gave Kelly a sick feeling in the pit of her stomach to know she'd killed someone, but if she hadn't, Jameson, Hank and she could have been murdered.

"Don't kill me," the gunman yelled, attempting to hold up his hands. Hard to do, though, with his injuries.

Kelly had been right about the gunshot wounds. They didn't appear life-threatening, but he was bleeding and needed medical attention. That wouldn't be difficult to get since they were in a hospital parking lot, but Gabriel likely wouldn't let any of the medical staff approach until he was certain it was safe.

Even though Kelly knew Jameson wasn't going to like it, she started to make her way toward them. She did keep low, though, crouching, and her pace wasn't exactly fast since she was still unsteady.

When Jameson spotted her, he didn't curse, but she could tell that's what he wanted to do. "Stay behind cover," he warned her.

She did, but that didn't stop her from getting a better look at the gunman that the deputy was now cuffing. Just as everyone else she'd encountered, Kelly didn't recognize him, but when the man looked in her direction, he did something strange.

He smiled at her.

Jameson and Gabriel noticed that smile, too,

because they both shifted their attention to her. "You know him?" Jameson asked her.

Kelly immediately shook her head. But the man just kept on smiling.

"I know you," the injured gunman growled, "because you're the woman who hired me."

Chapter Five

"I didn't hire that hit man," Kelly insisted.

Jameson had lost count of how many times Kelly had said a variation of that denial, but it had started immediately after the gunman's accusation. It had continued, too, even after the man had been hauled away to the ER and after she and Jameson arrived at the sheriff's office.

As with her other denials, no one responded. The two deputies who weren't at the hospital working the investigation were both busy at their desks. Gabriel was in the interview room with the driver who'd first seen Kelly and the two dead guys in the pasture. That left Jameson, and even though he, too, was on the phone, waiting for an update from Cameron, he wasn't there to give her any assurances but rather to make sure she didn't run.

Good thing, because she certainly looked like a woman on the verge of taking off.

She was pacing across the squad room. Well,

her version of pacing anyway, considering she was still wobbly. She would occasionally catch on to desks and chairs to steady herself.

Thankfully, she hadn't been so shaky that she hadn't managed to take out the female shooter in the hospital door. If she hadn't, the woman could have done some serious damage. It was that shot that had Jameson believing that the injured gunmen had been lying.

He stopped, rethought that.

Actually, he hadn't believed it from the moment he'd heard it. And yeah, that made him stupid. It was this old fire that was between Kelly and him. She'd stolen the file from him, but it was a huge leap to go from that to murder.

Kelly glanced down at the burner cell phone she had gripped in her hand. One of the deputies had given it to her after she said she wanted to make some calls. Of course, the calls had been related to her sister. Kelly hadn't remembered any phone numbers—or so she'd claimed—so Jameson had given her a contact at SAPD. The detective had nothing new on Mandy but promised to call Kelly the moment he found anything.

Jameson hoped what they didn't find was a body.

Kill Jameson Beckett or you'll never see her again.

That wasn't exactly a reassurance that Kelly's kid sister was okay.

She went to the watercooler and had another drink. Her third in the past hour. Jameson had already had her doctor come to the sheriff's office to check her and finish his exam, but Kelly had practically dismissed the man. Too bad. Because Jameson was certain that head injury needed additional treatment. Probably even a night or two in the hospital. He doubted, though, that he was going to be able to convince Kelly to go back there after what'd happened.

They'd nearly been killed.

It'd been pure luck that both Kelly and he had managed to nail those shots. And they'd managed that before the thugs had gotten their own brand of luck and killed all three of them and anyone else who happened to get in the path of those bullets.

Jameson finished his call with Cameron and went closer to her. The doctor had told him to watch her for any signs of dizziness or fatigue. He didn't see either. However, Jameson did see the troubled look on her face.

"I didn't hire that man," she repeated. Except this time, there were tears in her eyes.

Hell. The tears were his Achilles' heel, and Jameson had to force himself not to pull her into his arms. That definitely wouldn't be a good idea.

She stared at him as if waiting for something. A response, maybe. Maybe that hug. But instead Jameson relayed what he'd just learned from Cameron.

"No ID's on either the dead man or woman," he explained. "But Cameron took their prints and will see if they're in the system. I called in the Rangers to assist on this. When I have the names, I'll definitely run them past you to see if they ring any bells."

Kelly nodded. "Good." She repeated both the one-word response and the nod, and she kept staring at him.

"What about the guy you shot?" she asked. "The one who lied and said he was working for me?" She hadn't needed to clarify that last part, but the renewed anger in her voice seemed to help with drying up those tears.

"He lawyered up, but we do have an ID on him. He gave his name to the doctor because apparently he has some allergies to certain meds and wanted the doc to access his records. His name is Coy McGill. Know him?"

"No." Kelly added a heavy sigh. "But he's trying to set me up. Please tell me you know that." She was clearly calling him on this.

"I do know that," he assured her. "The shot

that woman fired could have killed you. If you'd been the one who hired them, she would have kept her gun aimed at me. After all, I'm the one that someone wants dead."

"Yes," she said after a long pause. Their eyes met again. "Why?"

For a simple question, it encompassed a lot. With everything going through his head, he hadn't exactly had much quiet time to think, but he kept coming back to two things.

"It could be connected to my parents' murders. The anniversary is just two days away." That would mean someone obsessed with the case. It could be someone who wanted revenge for Travis being behind bars.

"It's possibly connected to one of your cases," Kelly provided.

He had to nod again. As a Texas Ranger, he had made his share of enemies, and there were at least a half dozen guys behind bars who would want him dead. But this felt, well, personal.

"Why use you to do this?" Jameson was talking more to himself than her now.

She groaned softly, but it looked as if she wanted to curse. "I don't know, and that's why I need to remember."

"Then you should let the doctor examine

you again. Maybe there's something he can
give you—"

"He can't. I asked," she added. "He can rule
out a brain injury with tests, but even if that
is what's wrong with me, the only treatment
is time."

Jameson had no idea if the doctor had actually told her that or if it was something Kelly
had decided was true. Either way, he couldn't
force her. But he could force her into custody.

"Until Coy McGill starts talking, I can't let
you leave," Jameson spelled out for her.

"Because I'm a suspect," she readily supplied.

Great. That brought back the tears. They
shimmered in her eyes along with tugging at
his heart. And Jameson finally caved in and
gave her arm a gentle rub. She noticed, too. She
looked down at his hand. Then at him.

And there it came.

That old punch to the gut. Jameson had been
with plenty of women, but none of them had
ever made him feel the way Kelly had.

And that's why he took a huge step back
from her.

She noticed what he'd done, and the corner of
her mouth lifted. A smile, sort of, but it wasn't
from humor.

"Plus, you can't let me leave because Boyer

is still threatening that arrest warrant against me," Kelly added a moment later.

Bingo. There were a lot of pieces in this mess that didn't make sense, and Boyer was just one of them.

The door to the interview room finally opened, and Gabriel came out with the witness, a man named Merrill Stover. He wasn't a local but rather had been to a nearby ranch to look at some calves that were for sale. Jameson had run a background check on the man while Kelly was with the doctor, and Stover had a squeaky-clean record. No indications whatsoever that he'd had part in whatever the heck had gone on in that pasture.

Stover started for the door but stopped when he saw Kelly. "Ma'am, I'm real sorry for what happened to you."

Kelly pulled back her shoulders. "What *did* happen to me?"

Stover glanced back at Gabriel, but he waved off the question. "I'll fill her in. You're free to go," Gabriel assured him.

The man gave a suit-yourself shrug and left. Gabriel didn't say a word until he was out the door.

"I believe what he told me," Gabriel started. "But before you ask," he added to Kelly when she opened her mouth, "he didn't see the actual shooting. Only the aftermath of it."

She gave another of those weary sighs and scrubbed her hand over the back of her neck. "So I'm not cleared. Boyer can arrest me."

"No, he can't," Gabriel assured her. "Well, not without a court order, which I seriously doubt he'll get. That's because those two dead men aren't agents as he claimed. They both had long rap sheets."

Finally, Jameson saw some relief on her face. It was short-lived, though. "Why would Boyer claim they were agents?" she asked.

Gabriel lifted his shoulder. "I tried to call him, but he didn't answer. I left him a message."

Kelly leaned against the wall, and her eyelids fluttered a little. Jameson silently cursed. She was probably dizzy, something he was supposed to be watching for. Not that she'd ever admit it. However, she didn't balk when he took her by the arm and led her to a chair in Gabriel's office.

"Why would those men attack me?" She touched her fingers to her head.

"I don't know." Gabriel sounded as frustrated about that as Jameson was.

But Jameson had a theory. "Let's say someone wanted me dead and decided to use you to do that. You're not a thug or hired gun, but you've got the skill set to do the job since you're a PI. To force you to do this, they kidnap your sister."

That put some tears back in her eyes. Still, this was something Kelly needed to hear. It was something he needed to say aloud, too, to see if it made sense.

"They would keep your sister alive because that's the only leverage they have over you," Jameson reminded her. Now, here was the sticky part. "But something went wrong with their plan. You could have refused to do the hit on me, and the person behind this sent those two men after you. When they found you, you killed them in self-defense."

"Self-defense," she repeated in a whisper. Obviously, Kelly was trying to work this out, as well. She looked at Gabriel. "Did the two men have any kind of defensive wounds on them?"

"None. Only the gunshots that killed them. The shots came from your gun. We got the test results back on that," Gabriel added. "And you had gunshot residue on your hands."

Kelly stayed quiet a moment. "You think that's enough to convince Boyer to back off?"

"I hope so. Because I want you here in our custody at least until SAPD finds your sister."

Yeah, and it'd be a good idea to keep her

until that head injury was healed enough so she could tell them what was going on. Whenever the heck that would be.

"We probably haven't seen the last of Boyer," Jameson said. "He could be trying to figure out another reason to arrest you. Do you remember if you trust him?"

"No specific memories," she answered without hesitation. "But I don't trust him." She didn't hesitate with that, either.

Kelly's lack of trust definitely put Gabriel and him between a rock and a hard place. They wanted to cooperate with fellow law enforcement, but things weren't right here. Maybe Kelly had done something to Boyer and now he wanted to get back at her?

Jameson didn't get a chance to speculate more about that because he heard a familiar voice in the squad room. "Where the hell is the sheriff?" the man snarled.

Kelly practically bolted from the chair. "Who is that?"

"It's August Canton," Gabriel answered. "I called him in for questioning. I figured since you'd worked for him, seeing him might trigger some memories. I also want to ask him about the attacks."

Gabriel and Jameson stepped out in the hall

to face their visitor, and Kelly was right behind them.

It was August all right, but Jameson hadn't had any doubts about that. August made regular visits to the sheriff's office, and even though Jameson worked in San Antonio, he still managed to run into the man.

"That's August?" Kelly whispered. "When you said he was Travis's brother, I thought he'd be older. Thought he'd look different, too."

"He's Travis's half brother and only a few years older than Gabriel and me. As for the looks, well, he doesn't dress like most ranchers." More like a magazine version of a rancher in his designer clothes.

August was the offspring of his father's second marriage, and when his parents had been killed in a car crash when he was twelve, Travis had raised him. Jameson figured August always thought of Travis as more of a father than a half brother. That was probably why he was always fighting to get Travis out of jail.

And August had the money to keep up the fight, too.

Jameson didn't know the man's net worth, but August had inherited a trust fund from his mother's family.

"You two really need to get another whipping boy," August snapped. "Because I'm damn tired of you hauling me in here every time something goes wrong in your lives. I can't help it if some folks just want you two in the grave."

It was the typical junk that August spouted, but there was some truth in it. Gabriel and he had plenty of criminals who wanted to do them harm. But August had motive, too, because he blamed them for Travis's being convicted of the murders.

August looked ready to launch into more of that tirade, but he stopped when his attention landed on Kelly. The anger and tension dissolved from his expression, and he went to her, pulling her into his arms. The tension definitely didn't dissolve from Kelly. She went board-stiff.

"Are you okay?" August asked, leaning back enough so he could make eye contact with her.

She shook her head. "Someone tried to kill me. *Us*," Kelly corrected, motioning toward Jameson.

"Yes, I heard, and I'm sorry." August sounded genuine about that. *Sounded*. "I heard you lost your memory, too? I saw a nurse at the gas station, and she was talking about it."

Kelly nodded and eased back farther from him. Her forehead bunched up. "I don't remember you, but Jameson said you hired me and my sister to find something to clear your brother's name."

"I did. You both looked very hard but didn't find anything." August glanced at Jameson. "You don't think that had anything to do with someone trying to kill Kelly?" But he didn't wait for an answer. "I've told you all along that the real killer is out there, that my brother is innocent. The real killer probably thinks Kelly found something and wants to silence her."

Jameson didn't know whose huff was louder, his or Gabriel's. "Kelly worked for you two years ago," Jameson reminded the man. "If there is a *real killer* and he truly thought Kelly was a threat, why wouldn't he have gone after her back then?"

"I don't know. But it's your job to find out." August cursed. "How many more people are going to have to die or be put in danger before you reopen my brother's case and find the truth? And that truth is he's an innocent man."

Jameson didn't even bother to groan that time. They'd rehashed this argument so often that it no longer got much of a rise out of him.

"Do you know where Mandy is?" Kelly asked August. "Have you heard from her?"

"No," August said, sounding surprised. "What happened to her?"

"I'm not sure, but there were signs of a struggle in her apartment. And blood." Kelly's voice cracked when she said that last word.

August patted her arm much the way Jameson had earlier. Jameson didn't want to feel that coil of jealousy go through him. But he did.

Hell.

He really needed to find a way past these unwanted feelings for Kelly. She wasn't his, and it needed to stay that way.

"I'll make some calls and see if I can find out anything about your sister," August told her.

"The cops are doing that," Jameson snapped.

It was a knee-jerk reaction whenever he was around August. It came from all those years Gabriel and he had had to deal with August's claim that they'd arrested, and convicted, the wrong man for their parents' murders.

"And we know the cops never drop the ball on things," August grumbled back. When he turned to Gabriel, there wasn't a trace of the pleasantness that he'd shown Kelly. "Now, why don't you tell me why you summoned me here this time, and should I have brought my lawyer with me?"

"Did you do something illegal that would warrant your attorney being here?" Gabriel fired back. "I want to know if you had anything to do with hiring the thugs who tried to kill Jameson and Kelly."

"No. Of course not." August's eyes narrowed. "I have no reason to hurt Kelly. And I resent you insinuating that I did. Kelly and I are friends."

"Really?" Jameson questioned, and he didn't bother to sound sincere. "When's the last time you spoke to your *friend*?"

August turned that nasty expression on Jameson. "I haven't seen Kelly in a couple of years, but that doesn't mean I don't still consider her a friend. I want to help her. I want to keep her safe."

"We all want that," Jameson said. And he glanced at Kelly to see how she was handling this intense conversation.

Not well.

She was looking shaky again, and Jameson took hold of her arm to steady her. August didn't miss the gesture, and his mouth tightened. Heck, maybe the man was jealous, but it was just as likely that he didn't want to see his *friend* with a Beckett.

"If I'd known someone was after her," August continued a moment later, "I would have gotten in touch with her. With Mandy, too." His voice drifted off, because he turned in the direction of the front door that'd just opened.

Jameson and Gabriel looked there, too. And both probably had a similar reaction—they didn't need this now. But apparently they were going to get another visit from Boyer.

The agent's gaze went directly to them, and he walked toward them, flashing his badge to the deputy who tried to stop him.

"Hell," August muttered. "Why is he here?"

"You know him?" Gabriel asked August, and Jameson realized that with everything else going on, he hadn't filled his brother in on this.

"Yeah, and Agent Boyer knows me." August definitely didn't sound happy about that.

Boyer lifted an eyebrow. "And I know you. I'm investigating you for money laundering."

"For bilking Hattie Osmond out of a lot of money, too," Jameson added.

"It's all bogus." August didn't take his glare off the agent. "Are you here to harass me?"

"No, he's here to harass me," Kelly volunteered. "He thinks I murdered two thugs, but the truth is they were criminals, and I shot them in self-defense."

Boyer's gaze slashed to Jameson and Gabriel as if the agent expected them to confirm that. Jameson just settled for a nod. In light of the latest attack, Jameson was almost certain that's what'd happened.

Almost.

"You sure spend a lot of time fiddling in other people's business, Agent Boyer," August went on. "Seems to me you should be focusing on getting your own kid back."

That was yet something else Jameson hadn't had time to explain to Gabriel. And it probably didn't have anything to do with this case anyway. August was just muddying the waters by tossing it out there. He was also riling Boyer, and it'd obviously hit a nerve. The veins on Boyer's neck were practically bulging.

"I'll deal with you later," Boyer told August, and it sounded like a threat. "For now, I need to deal with her." He tipped his head to Kelly.

"What do you mean by that?" Kelly asked before Jameson could speak. She sounded a lot stronger than he knew she was. After all, she was practically leaning on him. "I've told you I'm innocent."

"But you don't know that, do you? In fact, you don't know much of anything right now because of this so-called amnesia."

"I know you're not taking her without an arrest warrant," Jameson said, "and you're not going to get one because you don't have enough evidence against her."

"We'll see about that." Again, it sounded like a threat, and Jameson doubted the man would just give up.

Kelly let out a long breath after Boyer walked out, but she kept her eyes on him until he was no longer in sight. "I wish I could remember what I did to make him come after me like this."

"You don't know?" August asked, but it wasn't exactly a question. It was an isn't-it-obvious tone.

The three of them just stared at August, and Jameson motioned for him to continue.

August did after he huffed. "Boyer believes Kelly has his little girl stashed away somewhere. And he'll do anything to force Kelly to give him back the child."

Chapter Six

Kelly jolted herself out of the dream. Or rather the nightmare. Images of gunmen trying to kill her.

Other images, too.

Before she opened her eyes, she could see some of the images. Watery bits of colors. Faces. Some of those faces were of her attackers, but one of them belonged to Mandy. Even though Kelly still didn't have any real memories of Mandy, she was certain that it was her kid sister.

That brought on the ache that was already heavy in her heart. Her sister was missing, and she wasn't able to help her. Mandy could be hurt. Dying. And here she was safe. For the moment anyway. But Kelly didn't exactly feel welcome here.

That's because she was in the guest room at Jameson's house on his family's ranch.

Jameson didn't want her at his place. Actually, he didn't want to be with her at all. She knew that. However, they hadn't exactly had a lot of options, considering he wanted to keep her close in case she remembered something that could help them unravel the reason behind the two attacks.

She checked the time on the clock, nearly 6:00 a.m., so Kelly got up and used the shower in the en suite bath. Her muscles were sore and stiff, but the pain was minor compared to her head. She was tempted to take some of the meds the doctor had given her after the exam at the sheriff's office, but she was afraid the pills would dull her memories even more.

She dressed, changing into the clothes Jameson had left for her the night before. The jeans and shirt were loaners from his sister Ivy, and they were much needed, too, since Kelly's own clothes had been covered with blood. She wasn't sure she would have been able to put them back on.

When she was done with the clothes, she made the mistake of looking in the mirror, and the jolt of seeing herself was as bad as the nightmare. That's because it was a stranger staring back at her.

Kelly touched her fingers to the bandage on her head. Whoever had hit her had probably been trying to kill her. Not exactly a thought to settle her queasy stomach. But what the person had done was take away who she was. Her name was Kelly Stockwell, but there were just a few traces of herself now. That had to change.

But how?

That question was repeating in her mind when she heard the footsteps. Kelly automatically reached for her gun—which she didn't have. She'd had the security guard's backup weapon during the hospital attack, but Jameson had arranged for it to be returned to the man. Too bad. Because she might need it now.

Or not.

There was a knock at the door, and a moment later Jameson opened it. "I heard you up," he said.

Not exactly a warm greeting, but there was some warmth when he looked her over. Unwanted warmth, no doubt. He stood with his forehead bunched up as if waiting for something. But that's when Kelly realized she hadn't buttoned the shirt. Her bare stomach and a skimpy white loaner bra were showing. She quickly fixed that and mumbled an apology.

"I don't have my memory back yet," Kelly volunteered just to get that out of the way.

He made a sound, a rumble deep in his chest that could have meant anything. "There's coffee."

Kelly didn't know if she drank it or not, but

she followed him to the kitchen and poured herself a cup. She tried it black, winced and heard Jameson make another sound. Maybe amusement this time.

"I guess that proves you're not faking the memory loss." He slid a small bowl her way. "You'll want three or four spoons of sugar in that."

She added three, sipped, then dumped in the fourth. Yes, that tasted right. It didn't surprise her that they'd obviously had coffee together. However, she was a little surprised that Jameson remembered how she took it. Maybe he'd had trouble erasing her from his mind—something that Kelly was certain he would like to do.

"Anything on my sister?" she asked. She sat at the table. Jameson didn't, though. With his coffee in hand, he went to the window to look out.

"Sorry, no. But the cops and Rangers are looking." He had a sip of his coffee before he said anything else. "I found out that August hired a couple of PIs to investigate Boyer. Not just Boyer's professional life, but his missing daughter, as well."

She could have sworn her heart skipped a beat. "Please tell me I didn't really take his child." Because even though she didn't remember August, Kelly had hoped that the man was wrong about that.

Jameson lifted his shoulder. "Boyer might truly believe you had something to do with it, but there's no proof that you did."

Thank goodness. That was something, at least. Though if she had done something like that, at least it would have been motive for Boyer to come after her. But then she had to shake her head.

"If Boyer is behind the attacks, why would he have coerced me into killing you?" Kelly asked.

"Maybe to throw suspicion off himself." Jameson answered it so quickly that he'd almost certainly given it plenty of thought. "This way, it would look as if this were between you and me and not between you and him."

Yes, and if he blamed her for taking his child, he would want revenge. Well, maybe. "He couldn't risk killing me if he believes I know where the child is," she pointed out. "Yet those gunmen seemed to have orders to eliminate us."

The moment Kelly said that, something hit her. And it wasn't something good.

"If Mandy also knew the location of the child," she went on, "she could have told Boyer. Then he wouldn't need me around. Or Mandy."

It suddenly felt as if someone had clamped a fist around her heart and kept squeezing. Her sister was at the mercy of someone who wanted her dead.

"Don't," Jameson said. "Boyer isn't our only suspect. August could have forced you to kill me because he hates me for putting Travis behind bars. He could have used you to do that."

True. But even if this was just directed at Jameson, it didn't help. Obviously, someone was after both of them. Heck, maybe Jameson's entire family.

"I've been looking for a possible money trail for the person who hired those thugs," Jameson went on. "I managed to get court orders for both Boyer and August."

Jameson had been busy. And lucky. Kelly figured it wasn't easy to get a court order for a federal agent's financials. "What did you find?"

"Nothing on Boyer, but then he could have some offshore or hidden accounts. Also he could have cash stashed away. A lot of it. He got a lawsuit settlement a while back for a car accident involving a drunk driver."

Having cash wasn't a good thing in this case, because they'd never know if Boyer had used it to hire hit men. Or kidnap Mandy.

"August is a different story," he went on. "Because of the attacks and threats that have been going on for the past couple of months, we've been keeping an eye on his financials. He's rich, by the way. A huge trust fund that he taps into regularly to pay for attorneys and PIs to clear his brother's name."

Yes, and she'd apparently been one of those PIs.

"The money trail definitely leads to August, but it's almost too obvious," Jameson quickly added. "The funds came from an offshore account that was set up just last week. I'm sure August will say that it's bogus, and it'll be hard to prove that it's not."

Especially since someone with Boyer's federal connections could have easily done something like that. But that led Kelly to something else that she'd considered.

"Is it possible that when I was working for August I uncovered something that would, well, incriminate August himself?" she asked.

"Maybe. The file you stole from me had plenty about him in it, including my personal notes."

She remembered Boyer and him talking about this. Jameson had considered August a suspect in his parents' murders because Jameson's father had been investigating August at the time. But maybe she had used whatever was in that file to lead her to something else.

Like August's guilt.

That could possibly explain why she'd disappeared two years ago. Of course, the obvious reason she'd left was because Jameson hated her for stealing that file. She hated herself for doing it, too. Kelly hoped when her memories returned that there was a better reason for her taking it other than her just doing her job.

And that brought her back to what was happening now.

If August was connected to the attacks, then the motive had to go back to the file. Or maybe to what'd happened ten years ago.

"Did Travis admit to killing your parents?" she asked. But Kelly wished she hadn't. Jameson's long, weary breath told her this was a topic that was still picking away at those old wounds he had.

"No. He was an alcoholic and had blackouts. Like you, he has memory issues."

That sounded a little like a dig, but she couldn't blame him. If Travis remembered what happened that night, then it might help them solve who was behind the attacks.

"Part of me wishes it weren't Travis," Jameson continued a moment later. "Because Travis's son and daughter are involved with my brother and sister."

Yes, that did create some bad family dynamics. Of course, maybe Travis's children hated their father for what he'd done. The Beckett murders had certainly created a lot of pain and suffering for those who'd been left behind.

Heck, it was still creating it because of those threats Jameson had mentioned and the attacks.

"You have someone protecting your sisters?" Kelly asked.

He nodded. "Ivy's engaged to a DEA agent, Theo. He won't let anything happen to her. They're staying at Gabriel's for now with him and his wife, Jodi. My other sister, Lauren, is engaged to Cameron, the deputy who works here."

Kelly figured she'd met these people. Or at least had known about them. But that, too, was lost in the jumble of memories.

"Even if your sisters are being protected, it's too dangerous for me to stay here," she reminded him. "In fact, I probably shouldn't be anywhere near you."

He glanced at her, his eyebrow raised. Maybe he'd taken that the wrong way. As in she shouldn't be near him because of the attraction, but his eyebrow lowered just as quickly.

"Once I get an update from Gabriel, we'll weigh the options," he answered. "Plus, you should probably go back to the hospital and press the doctor to see if he can do anything about your amnesia."

"No. Not after what happened. Besides, the doctor ran tests." Of course, those test results hadn't told her what she needed to know— would her memory ever return? Or would she be like this forever?

Jameson kept his attention pinned out the window, which made her wonder just how long he'd been keeping watch. Hopefully, not all night. Though that might explain why he was drinking the coffee like water. He poured himself another cup and went right back to the window.

Kelly joined him so she could get a better look at the place. When they'd arrived the night before, it'd already been too dark for her to see much. However, she certainly saw it now. The ranch was huge.

"All of this is Beckett land?" she asked.

"Yeah. My great-grandfather originally bought it and passed it down the generations. When my folks died... Gabriel, Ivy, Lauren and I inherited it."

He paused over the word *died*, and she noticed the sudden tightness of his jaw. His parents' murders were obviously still a raw wound.

Kelly leaned closer to the window so she could see the road that led up from a large house. Gabriel's, probably. There was also a house on the other side of the property, but it clearly wasn't occupied and appeared to have some recent damage.

"We had a fire last month," Jameson said, following her gaze. "Someone tried to go after my sister and her fiancé."

So the Becketts weren't new to attacks. But that still didn't mean Kelly should be there to bring more danger to their doorsteps.

"We've been getting threats for a while now," he went on. "There's been some press about the anniversary of the murders, and that sometimes brings out the lunatics and copycats."

"It's a shame because, despite everything, this is still your home." She paused. "Did you bring me here when we, uh, were seeing each other?"

He nodded, then drank more of his coffee. "Remember anything about it?"

Kelly glanced around the large open kitchen and living room. There was nothing familiar. So she closed her eyes to try again. Some images came. Fast and blurry. As she'd done with the nightmare, she tried to pick through them. And she finally did.

"You have a tattoo," Kelly blurted out, and she looked at his shoulder. She couldn't see the tat, of course, because he was wearing a shirt, but if her memory was right, it was a dragon.

Another nod to verify the tat. But he didn't verify anything else about it. Especially the fact that he would have had to be partially undressed for her to have seen it.

Jameson finally turned to her, but it wasn't exactly a loving look he gave her. He checked her bandage. Frowned. And gave it a slight adjustment. Of course, for that to happen, he had to touch her. His fingertips brushed against her skin, and the shiver went through her.

Kelly stepped back. And Jameson noticed. He probably noticed her reaction to him, as well. He stared at her as if he was about to say something, but then his phone rang, the sound shooting through the room. He touched her again, moving her back from the window, before he set aside his coffee and took his phone from his pocket.

"It's Gabriel," he said. Jameson hit the answer button and put the call on speaker. "Kelly's next to me," he added to his brother.

She hoped that didn't cause Gabriel to hold back something he might have said, but the sheriff's long pause told her that he would probably at least try to soften any bad news.

"McGill, the gunman, is finally talking," Gabriel explained, "but he's still insisting it was Kelly who hired him."

"He's lying," she repeated.

Neither man had a reaction to that, and Gabriel just continued. "I offered him a plea deal. He'd have to give me proof that it was Kelly who hired him, and in exchange I'd ask the DA for lesser charges. McGill didn't go for it."

"Maybe because he figures he's a dead man if he says anything," Jameson quickly provided. "Or else there's no proof to be found."

Kelly groaned. She hated to think there was nothing out there that could clear her name. "Maybe someone made McGill believe I was the one behind it," she suggested. "Maybe someone posing as me through phone conversations and such." It couldn't have been a face-to-face pretense, though, because McGill had gotten a close look at her in the hospital parking lot.

"That's my guess, too," Gabriel agreed. "Of course, he could have a more personal stake in this. Perhaps someone kidnapped a family member or his boss could be a friend. We're looking into any connections between McGill, August and Boyer."

Good. Because if they could make a link like that, it would put a quicker end to this investigation.

"I did talk to a few of Boyer's fellow agents," Gabriel added, "and, yeah, he does believe Kelly assisted in taking his daughter. Apparently, Kelly knew Boyer's ex, Hadley, and Boyer believes Hadley convinced Kelly to help her take the child."

"But why? Was Boyer abusive?" Kelly asked.

"Not according to anyone I spoke with, but no one had anything good to say about Hadley. People agreed that she was controlling and manipulative. She could have maybe made you believe that the baby and she were in danger. That could explain why you would do something like that."

Yes, it could. However, Kelly still couldn't remember Hadley or this baby. She forced herself to think, to try to sort through those memory fragments again. This time, she got a too-clear image of Jameson.

Naked.

It was so clear that she made a sound of surprise. A sound that certainly got Jameson's attention. "What is it?" he demanded.

She waved him off and was about to lie and say it was nothing, but another image came. Not of Jameson this time.

But of a baby.

A little girl with dark hair, and she was smiling. The image came and went in a flash, but it was just as clear as the one of Jameson.

"Oh, God." Kelly touched her fingers to her mouth. Both her mouth and hand were trembling now. "I might have taken her."

Jameson stared at her. Gabriel cursed. "What do you remember?" Gabriel snapped.

"Nothing other than seeing her in my mind. I can't recall anything about kidnapping her."

"You might not have," Jameson said. "It's possible Hadley brought her to you."

True. But where was the child now? Hadley was dead, and Kelly instinctively knew there was no way she'd leave the child alone.

"Maybe you can put out an APB for the little girl," Kelly suggested.

"There's already an Amber Alert," Gabriel explained, "but the Rangers have stepped up efforts to find her." He paused, and she could hear him talking to someone else in the background. "The emergency dispatcher just called, and he said he has Mandy on the line."

Kelly's heart dropped. She put her coffee cup on the windowsill and practically snatched the phone from Jameson. "Where is she? Is she okay?" Kelly's words were so fast that they ran together.

"I'll have the call transferred here," Gabriel

said, "but I have to put you on hold for a second to do that."

"Mandy's alive," Kelly whispered while she waited. That didn't mean her sister was okay, though.

The seconds suddenly seemed like hours, and Kelly's hand only shook harder. So hard that Jameson finally pried the phone from her but held it so that she wouldn't have any trouble hearing.

"Kelly?" someone finally said from the other end of the line.

She didn't recognize the voice, but Kelly looked at Jameson and he nodded. "It's your sister."

"Kelly," Mandy repeated. "I can't stay on the line or they'll find me. God, Kelly, you have to come and get me now. I'm bleeding, and I'm not sure how much longer I can run from those men. Please, just come right now."

Chapter Seven

Jameson wanted to curse. Because that wasn't a good thing to hear Kelly's sister say.

I'm bleeding, and I'm not sure how much longer I can run from those men.

But it was better than the alternative. He hadn't come out and said it to Kelly, but he'd figured Mandy was dead. And she soon might be if what she'd just said was true. Just in case it wasn't or if this was some kind of ploy to draw out Kelly, Jameson fired off a text to Gabriel so he could try to trace the call.

"Remember, the kidnappers could be forcing her to say whatever she's about to say to you," Jameson told Kelly.

She shook her head, maybe not believing that. Probably because she didn't want to believe it. "Are you okay?" she asked her sister.

"No. I told you, I'm bleeding. I've been shot."

There went the rest of the color in Kelly's face. "Oh, God. How bad?"

Jameson wanted to know that, but more important, he needed to find out where to send the cops and an ambulance. "This is Jameson Beckett," he said to Mandy. "Where are you?"

Silence. Several long moments of it. That silence put a knot in Jameson's stomach.

"I'm not sure," Mandy finally said. "A day ago, two armed thugs took me and have been holding me in some kind of warehouse. When they weren't watching, I managed to get out of the ropes they used to tie my hands. I stole one of their phones and started running. That's when one of them shot me."

Jameson would need to hear a lot more details about that, but it could wait. "Where are you?" he repeated.

"I, uh, think I'm just outside of San Antonio."

If she was, then Gabriel should be able to find her. Well, unless she was using a burner phone. "Look around you," he instructed just in case it was an untraceable prepaid phone. "Do you see any landmarks, anything familiar?"

There was a rattle of static from the other end of the line, but he could also hear Mandy's heavy gusts of breath. "There's a road. Not an interstate, but I can see some buildings in the distance. No cars, though. Please, just come and get me. It's not safe here. Those men could find me."

Yeah, they probably could. "I have someone tracing the call," he assured her. "Just stay put and if there's anywhere you can hide, do it. Also, how bad are you bleeding?"

"It's my arm. There's blood on my sleeve and shirt."

Jameson felt some relief. An arm wound wouldn't necessarily be fatal unless they couldn't find her in time. If they didn't, she might bleed out.

"Try to clamp your hand over the wound," he told her. "It should slow the bleeding."

"I just need you to come," Mandy begged. "Kelly, *please*. You told me if anything went wrong that you'd help me."

"And I will help you," Kelly assured her. "But I've been hurt, too. A head injury. I have amnesia."

"What?" Mandy repeated that, the disbelief easy to hear in her voice. "When did this happen?"

"Last night. Maybe a few hours after you were kidnapped." Kelly's expression was already troubled, and it stayed that way. "While Gabriel's tracing your call, maybe you can tell me why I was carrying around a note that said for me to kill Jameson?"

Mandy made a sharp sound of surprise. "I don't know." The static crackled through the line. "Obviously, you didn't kill him if he's with you now."

"No. But some men came after us. I need to know why someone would have sent me after Jameson."

Mandy hesitated again. "Maybe the same reason those goons took me, but I don't know that reason." More static. "Where are Jameson and you right now?"

Jameson shook his head when Kelly started to answer. "Someone could be listening to Mandy's conversation to figure out where you are so he or she can send more gunmen," he whispered to Kelly.

Her eyes widened, and she nodded. Of course, there were people who already knew that he'd brought Kelly here, but Jameson didn't want to hand over that information to possible would-be killers.

"Look around you again," Kelly said to Mandy a moment later. "Try to figure out where you are."

No answer. Just static. "I have to go," Mandy finally answered, her words were whispered but rushed together. "I'll call you when I can."

"Wait—" But Kelly was talking to herself because her sister had already ended the call. "Mandy!" she shouted into the phone.

A hoarse sob tore from Kelly's mouth, and she sagged against him. "We have to find her."

"Gabriel should have the phone trace done in a few minutes." Jameson hoped so anyway, and maybe his brother would be able to pinpoint Mandy's exact location.

"We should just start driving," Kelly insisted. "We could head toward San Antonio—"

"No." This wasn't going to be an easy thing to tell her, nor an easy thing for Kelly to hear, and he slipped his arm around her. "All of this could be a trap to get to you."

She dropped her head on his shoulder, but just as quickly, it came back up, and she stared at him. "You don't think my sister is the one after me?"

"No." He didn't know of any reason why Mandy would do that. Of course, there was plenty about this investigation that he didn't know. "But the kidnappers could have allowed her to escape so they could use her to draw you out."

"Why would they have shot her then?" she asked.

Good question, and Jameson had some bad answers. "Maybe she wasn't shot. They could have told her to say that."

Kelly was shaking her head before he even

finished. "I might not remember Mandy, but she's my sister."

"Siblings do bad things to each other all the time." And Jameson wished he'd toned that down some. Still, it was true. "Think about it. Mandy called the Blue River emergency number. She must have known you were here. And how would she have known that if she didn't learn about it from the kidnappers?"

He watched as she processed that, and her mouth started to tremble. The tears came back to her eyes. Tears that tugged at him almost as much as this blasted attraction between them. Jameson didn't push her away, but it was something he should have done. Because he found himself brushing a kiss on her forehead. Definitely way too cozy and intimate, considering there was no way he wanted to go another emotional round with Kelly.

"It doesn't mean Mandy wants to hurt you," he added. He pulled back, meeting her eye to eye. "In those memory fragments, you're not remembering anything about how Mandy is involved in this, are you?"

"No." She blinked back tears and wiped away the one that had spilled down her cheek. "But you're wondering why she said what she did. *You told me if anything went wrong that you'd help me.*"

Bingo. "There must have been some kind of plan. One that clearly involved her. One that had the possibility for danger if there was something that could go wrong."

She nodded. "Maybe something to do with Boyer. Probably to do with his child." Kelly looked away from him. "I keep seeing glimpses of a baby, and if I took her… God, Jameson. She could be in danger, too."

Yeah, and that was only the tip of the iceberg. Kelly could be charged with kidnapping and sent to jail. But if Boyer wanted revenge, he could kill her long before she made it behind bars.

His phone rang, causing her to gasp and reach for it. Probably because Kelly thought it was her sister. But it was Gabriel's name on the screen. Jameson jabbed the answer button as fast as he could and put the call on speaker.

"No trace on Mandy's call," Gabriel said right away. "It was a burner."

Jameson tried not to let his expression show that it was a devastating blow. That's because it hit Kelly as hard as he figured it would. This time, though, she didn't lean on him. She groped behind her to find the chair and dropped down into it. She buried her face in her hands and was no doubt crying again.

"Mandy did tell the dispatcher that she'd put

the phone on silent because she didn't want her kidnappers to hear the ringing. That way, if you do call her back, at least the men after her won't be able to hear it."

That was a good precaution to take. One he was surprised that Mandy would remember considering she was on the run.

"Mandy thought she was outside of San Antonio," Jameson explained to his brother. "She said two men had been holding her in a warehouse. She was near a road."

"I'll give all of this to SAPD so they can start using traffic cameras to try to locate her. Just hang tight for now," Gabriel added before he ended the call.

Hanging tight was easier said than done. The moment Jameson put his phone away, Kelly got up and started to pace. She groaned softly, pushed her hair away from her face. And winced again. This time, though, it wasn't from hearing her sister. It was almost certainly because she'd brushed her fingers over her injury, and she was in pain.

"You could take some meds," he reminded her.

Kelly waved that off and kept pacing. "I have to try to help her," she said. "I can't just wait around here while something bad happens to Mandy."

Apparently the bad had already happened, but Jameson kept that to himself. He also continued to keep watch out the window. He'd alerted the ranch hands that there could be some trouble, but Jameson wanted to make sure none of those hired guns got anywhere on Beckett land, much less close enough to his house to fire some shots.

"Mandy and I must've planned something." Kelly seemed to be talking to herself now. Probably trying to work it out of her head. "She didn't know anything about that note I was carrying, the one that said I should kill you."

"No," Jameson agreed. "But maybe your plan didn't involve me. Not directly anyway. But that could have changed when the kidnappers took Mandy. You were obviously heading either here or Blue River when those two men attacked you."

And that led him right back to August, not Boyer. Because as far as Jameson knew, Boyer didn't have a reason to want him dead. He couldn't say the same for August. He really did need to get the man back in for questioning, and he could use the financial paper trail to do that. Of course, he'd interrogated August plenty of times and had rarely learned anything useful.

Well, except for August handing over Boyer on a silver platter by connecting the agent's missing daughter to Kelly. In this case, though, August might not have been blowing smoke.

"Tell me about the baby you've been recalling," he said. He didn't expect much, but maybe if he got Kelly's mind on something else, it would keep her from bolting for the door—something she looked as if she wanted to do.

She gave a heavy sigh. "Dark hair. Definitely a little girl because she's wearing a dress and smiling. Not a newborn. She's sitting up, in my lap, I think. In someone's lap anyway." Kelly squinted as if trying to give him more, but then she shook her head. "Sorry. That's all."

Definitely not much, but it was a good start. "Just keep focusing on it. If you don't have your memory back soon, I can get a sketch artist. That way, we can maybe do an age progression of photos of Boyer's daughter and see if they match."

"There are photos?" she asked.

"Yes. Ones taken shortly after she was born." And he wanted to kick himself for not showing them to her sooner. "I found them last night when I was looking into Boyer's personal life and his recent investigations." He tipped his head to the laptop. "I'm pretty sure I left the tab with the photos open."

Kelly hurried there while he stayed at the window, and Jameson volleyed glances between her and the road. Even though he couldn't see the computer screen, he knew the exact moment Kelly spotted them because she held her breath and leaned in closer to study them.

Jameson realized he was holding his breath, too. A lot was riding on whether or not she recognized that baby.

"I don't know," Kelly said several moments later. "The baby in my memory is older so I can't tell if the features are the same or not."

Jameson took out his phone again to text a Ranger friend about getting access to some age progression software, but before he could do that, he got a call from Gabriel. Kelly must have known it was important, and she went back to him.

"It's Mandy again," Gabriel explained. "She won't talk to me and is insisting on speaking to her sister. I'm transferring the call to you now."

As with the other call, it took Mandy several seconds to come onto the line. "I got away from them," she immediately said in a hoarse whisper. "But I don't know how soon they'll find me again."

"Where are you now?" Jameson asked.

"Put Kelly on the line," Mandy insisted.

"I'm here," Kelly assured her.

"Good. Because I doubt I'll have long to talk so listen carefully. I'm hiding in a warehouse.

There's no one here, but there are some boxes that say Carswell Shipping. I think that's the name of the place. I need you to come and get me, but don't call the cops."

Jameson had been about to text Gabriel with that info, but he stopped. "Why no cops?"

"Because I think the kidnappers have cop friends. Or hell, they could be cops themselves. Definitely some kind of law enforcement connections. I can tell that from the snatches of their conversations I've been able to overhear."

Jameson wanted to know more about those conversations, wanted to know more about a lot of things, but he would trust Mandy on this. For now.

"Gabriel's not on any kidnapper's payroll. Nor are his deputies," Jameson told her. "They can come and get you."

"No. I want Kelly and you. Only the two of you. I don't trust anyone but my sister."

"That can't happen," Jameson said at the exact moment when Kelly said, "We'll get there as fast as we can."

"Good." He could hear the relief in Mandy's voice. "Please hurry."

There was no way Jameson was going to agree to what Kelly had just assured her sister. "Mandy, someone's trying to kill Kelly. It's not safe for her to be at some warehouse looking for you. Especially when that might not even be the name of the place."

"I know, and I'm sorry. So sorry," Mandy repeated. It sounded as if she was crying now. "But please, just come."

Jameson shook his head when Kelly opened her mouth. No doubt to assure her sister they were on the way. He even took hold of Kelly's arm to make certain she didn't grab his keys and make a run for it.

"I'll come to you," Jameson finally said to Mandy, "but I'm leaving Kelly where it's safe." Which in this case would be the sheriff's office. No way would Jameson tell Mandy that, though.

"No, bring Kelly. You have to bring her. I won't trust anyone unless she's with them. And if you don't bring her, I'll just keep running."

Then Jameson heard something he didn't want to hear.

"Oh, God, they found me," Mandy whispered.

And that whisper was followed by the sound of gunfire.

Chapter Eight

"This is a mistake," Jameson said. He'd been repeating a variation of that since Mandy's second phone call.

Kelly figured he was right. It was a mistake, but she didn't have a choice. Just as Jameson hadn't had a choice to bring her along. Of course, he hadn't done it willingly, but she'd finally convinced him that one way or another she was going to get to her sister.

Apparently, she'd promised her sister that she would help her if anything went wrong. And something had. Now it was up to Kelly to try to make that right.

If that was possible.

She would hear the sound of that gunshot for the rest of her life. It had cut her to the bone. Since just thinking about it nearly caused a panic attack, Kelly reminded herself that Mandy could have gotten away from the men. After all, she'd managed to escape from them once, so perhaps she had been able to do it again.

"Mandy wouldn't have met with you if I hadn't been with you," Kelly pointed out to Jameson.

It also was a repeat, and they'd been hashing out the same argument since leaving for the Carswell Shipping warehouse on the outskirts of San Antonio. Not a long trip. Less than forty-five minutes, but each mile seemed like an eternity.

They hadn't followed Mandy's orders to a T, though. Yes, Kelly was with Jameson in a cruiser. Not alone. Cameron was driving it, and behind them was Gabriel and another deputy, Susan Bowie, in an unmarked car.

But that wasn't the only precautions Jameson had taken.

They were all wearing Kevlar vests, and SAPD would be nearby when they approached the warehouse. Jameson had insisted on backup. Had also insisted on her staying in the vehicle at all times.

"The ambulance will be there, too?" she asked.

Jameson nodded. "There'll be one with the SAPD officers." He looked at her. Except it was more of a glare. "You do know that this is a stupid idea."

"Yes, but I'd do plenty of stupid things to save my sister."

"You don't even remember her," he spat out. "Do you?"

"No. So far, the bits and pieces I'm remembering are of you and that baby."

Boyer's baby. Once Mandy was safe, then Kelly could find out where the child was and make sure she was safe, too. Because if those thugs had come after Mandy and her, they might go after the child, as well.

"Do you know of anything Mandy has ever done to make you distrust her?" Kelly came out and asked.

Jameson stayed quiet for a moment and then shook his head. "I didn't know her that well, and you never mentioned any concerns you had about her."

Judging from the flicker of his jaw muscles, there was something else he wanted to say. Something that Kelly wouldn't necessarily want to hear.

"I guess I'm troubled by the fact that Mandy would participate in a baby's kidnapping," he finally explained.

That meant he was troubled with her own participation in it, too. Well, welcome to the club. Kelly didn't even know who she was any longer, but it didn't sit well with her to have done something like that. Especially if she'd been duped into it by Hadley. Because if Boyer was right, Hadley had wanted the baby taken to get back at him.

"I'll try to call Mandy again," she said, taking the phone from Jameson. Kelly had lost count of how many times she'd done that. Had lost count of the prayers she'd been saying for her sister's safety. Not just from the kidnappers but also from the gunshot wound.

When she redialed the number, there was still no answer. That didn't mean her sister was dead, though. Mandy could have ditched or dropped the phone while she was running from her kidnappers. Plus, since Mandy's phone was on silent, she might not know about Kelly's repeated attempts to call her. Of course, Mandy had to know they would be trying to get in touch with her.

"When we get there, you won't leave this cruiser," Jameson reminded her. Since it was yet another bit of repeated info, she wasn't likely to forget it. Or find some way around it. Still, if Mandy could just see her from a distance, maybe that would be enough to draw her out.

First, though, Jameson, Gabriel and the deputies would have to make sure the kidnappers were no longer a threat.

"Keep trying to remember anything that will help us with this," Jameson added when he took back his phone. He also continued to keep watch around them.

Kelly was doing the same and considered pressing Jameson again to give her a weapon. He'd refused the other times she'd asked, but maybe once they got closer to the warehouse, he'd reconsider.

She didn't want to close her eyes for fear she would miss something, like someone following them. But Kelly did do as Jameson had said, and she tried to force those images and fragments back into her mind. Since there were so many pieces that didn't make sense, she tried to focus on the baby.

And she saw her again.

Smiling, wearing a pink dress. She was reaching up her hands as if she wanted someone to take her. Kelly looked past the child, hoping to figure out where she was. A room with white walls. It could have been any room in any house, because there were no other details for her to latch onto. Like the other memories, it was gone in a flash.

Replaced by a much more recent memory.

"You kissed me," she said. Though she certainly hadn't meant to say it aloud.

Jameson frowned when he turned toward

her. He didn't say a word, but there was a what-the-heck look in his eyes.

"When we were at the window at your house," she added. "You kissed my forehead." Since he was still frowning, Kelly waved that off. "Sorry."

The frown continued, added with some muttered profanity. "You caught me at a weak moment." He paused, said more of those under-the-breath curse words. "I have a history of weak moments when it comes to you."

For some stupid reason, that made her smile. Though it shouldn't have. It was obvious Jameson wanted things to be over between them. And they would be. As soon as they rescued her sister and caught the people responsible. Kelly desperately wanted those things to happen, but it gave her an empty feeling inside to realize that after this, she might never see Jameson again.

"Are you remembering something?" he asked. Maybe to change the subject or maybe because Kelly was certain her expression had changed. Definitely not a smile now.

She shook her head but didn't have to add more because Jameson's phone rang. Just like that, her heart was right back in her throat, but it wasn't her sister. Those calls had come through as Unknown Caller, but this one had the phone number. Jameson answered it, putting it on speaker, and Kelly immediately heard a familiar voice.

"What the hell's going on?" Boyer demanded.

"Plenty," Jameson snarled. "Did you have something specific you wanted to whine about?"

Even though Boyer didn't answer immediately, Kelly could practically feel the man seething with anger. "You know why I'm calling. It's Mandy. You found her."

Jameson's eyes narrowed, and she knew why. Someone had obviously leaked the info to Boyer. That shouldn't have surprised her since the SAPD cops were on scene. Kelly didn't remember how law enforcement communicated with each other, but it was possible Boyer had access to those communications' channels.

"Did we find her?" Jameson countered. "Because we're not sure exactly where she is."

"The warehouse," Boyer snapped.

"That's just a guess, and she's on the run from kidnappers. Mandy could be anywhere."

It was true. And that caused Kelly's chest to tighten even more.

"She's there," Boyer insisted. "And I soon will be, too. If you get to her first, find out if my daughter is with her."

Jameson didn't agree to that. "Just stay out

of the way," he added, and Jameson ended the conversation when his phone dinged to indicate he had another call coming in.

This time Unknown Caller was on the screen.

"Please tell me you're coming after me," Mandy said the moment that Jameson answered.

"We are if you're at the Carswell warehouse."

"I'm not. I had to get away from there. I'm about a quarter of a mile from there at a truck stop. I'm hiding behind the building."

Cameron immediately relayed that info to Gabriel.

"Do you have eyes on the kidnappers?" Jameson asked her.

"No, but they have to be nearby." Mandy made a sound that he thought might have been a muffled sob. "Please hurry."

"We will, but if you can, stay on the line in case you have to go on the move again."

"I'll try. Is Kelly with you?"

"Yes," Kelly answered, causing Jameson to give her another of those nasty glares.

She listened carefully for her sister's reaction, but there wasn't one. Not one that Kelly could hear anyway.

"Why did I tell you I'd help you if something went wrong?" Kelly pressed. "What exactly were we doing that had the potential to turn bad?"

"You honestly don't remember?"

"No. Just bits and pieces that don't make sense. Who's trying to kill me and why? And who kidnapped you?"

"I don't know." Her sister didn't hesitate that time. "But I think it all goes back to that file you took from Jameson. Do you remember someone trying to kill you after that?"

Heavens. She definitely hadn't remembered that. "No. Who?"

"I figured it was Jameson. Or someone in his family. That's why I didn't want to trust him or his brother."

Jameson cursed. "I didn't try to kill her. Neither did Gabriel."

"Well, someone did, and that's why you went on the run." Mandy made that low moan again. "I figured there was something in that file that someone wanted to keep secret."

Kelly thought that could be true, but if so, she still didn't believe Jameson was behind it. "Do you have the file?" Kelly asked her.

"No. You do."

Kelly's stomach sank. That was not what she wanted to hear. Because she had no idea where it was.

"How far out are you?" Mandy asked, the urgency in her voice going up even more.

"Less than five minutes," Cameron provided.

"Well, hurry, because I just spotted the thugs again. I have to go." And with that, her sister ended the call.

Cameron was already driving as fast as it was safe to go, but he pushed even harder on the accelerator.

"Your sister is smart," Jameson reminded Kelly. "She'll stay hidden until we're there. You're smart, too," he added without even hesitating. "That's why you'll stay put in this cruiser. Agreed?"

Kelly nodded. It was the smart and safe thing to do. She only hoped they didn't arrive to her sister being caught in the middle of a gunfight. Or worse. Mandy could be hurt even more than she already was.

"Once we've had a chance to question Mandy," Jameson went on, "she might be able to fill in some of your memory gaps."

He put away his phone, and because they were getting closer to the truck stop, he drew his weapon. Kelly hadn't needed a reminder of the danger, but that gave her another jolt anyway.

Another jolt of memory, too.

This time it wasn't the bits and pieces but a

full-fledged image. Of her running. It was so vivid she could feel her pulse throbbing, could hear her own ragged breath. There was a taste in her mouth, too, and it took her a moment to realize it was blood. She had blood in her mouth as well as on her face because she could feel it running down the side of her head.

"Are you okay?" Jameson asked. She heard the alarm in his voice, and he touched her arm.

Kelly tried to answer, but she was caught up in the images. So real. So painful. And the images kept coming. She stumbled, her body pitching forward, and she fell, landing on some damp grass. That's when she realized she was in a pasture.

No. *The* pasture.

The place where those men had attacked her and robbed her of her memory.

"It's not real," she said, repeating it so that it wouldn't cause her to have a panic attack. She had survived, more or less, and the memories and those men couldn't hurt her now.

But the reminder didn't work. More memories hit her. She saw the gun in her hand, felt the grass beneath her as she rolled over and came up ready to fire. If she didn't shoot, they would kill her. Kelly could see that cold, flat look on their faces. She was a job to them.

The one on the right took aim at her, but

Kelly pulled the trigger first. Her shot slammed into his chest. Before he even dropped to the ground, she put two bullets in the other one.

"I remember killing those men," Kelly managed to say. "I did it. I killed them."

Judging from the sound Jameson made, that hadn't surprised him. However, he kept staring at her, clearly waiting for more. But there wasn't more. The images faded just as quickly as they'd come.

"It's a start," he added. "For now, though, I need you to get down on the seat."

She snapped toward the window, and that's when Kelly saw the truck stop just ahead. Or at least she saw the trucks. There were five semis parked around the one-story building, and four men were milling near the front door.

No sign of Mandy, though.

She slid lower in the seat but kept her head high enough so she could hopefully glance out the front window, but Jameson pushed her down.

Then he cursed.

"I see Mandy," Jameson said, "and she's got a gun."

Kelly shook her head, certain he was wrong. Her sister hadn't said anything about a gun when she'd called them. "Maybe she took it from one of the kidnappers."

Of course, there could be another explanation. One that Kelly prayed wasn't true. That this was a trap and her sister had betrayed her.

"She's bleeding all right," Cameron added a moment later.

That got Kelly sitting up, and it didn't take her long to spot the woman peering around the back edge of the building. She had dark brown hair that was cut short and choppy. There was nothing familiar about her face. Nothing familiar about her. But there was indeed blood on the sleeve of her light blue shirt.

Her sister lifted her head, her attention going straight to the cruiser. She didn't move, though. Instead, she looked around, maybe for those goons who'd taken and injured her.

Cameron pulled the cruiser closer and stopped at the side of the building. He couldn't go any farther because of a Dumpster and several parked cars. Mandy was still a good ten feet away.

"If you get out of the cruiser, I'll arrest you," Jameson warned Kelly.

She didn't think he was bluffing, either. However, he got out. Before Kelly could tell him that it was too dangerous, he had the door open. He didn't go to her sister, though. He kept cover behind the door of the cruiser.

"Jameson," Mandy said. "Where's my sister?"

"Inside the car."

It was hard to tell from Mandy's expression if she was relieved about that. "And you're positive you can trust the cops you brought with you?"

"I trust them with my life," Jameson assured her. "And Kelly's."

Mandy hesitated as if deciding if that was true or not, but she finally did start toward them.

"You're not getting in the cruiser unless you give me that gun," Jameson ordered. And it was indeed an order. It stopped Mandy in her tracks. "When you come closer, hold the gun down by your side and don't make any sudden moves."

Mandy glanced at the gun as if debating that. Not good, because it was probably way too dangerous for her to be out there. Too dangerous for all of them. Even with Gabriel behind them and the San Antonio cops nearby, Mandy and Jameson could be cut down in a gunfight.

"If this is a trick, I'll make you pay," Mandy spat out like profanity. She followed it with some real profanity before she finally walked to Jameson.

He took the gun from her, tucking it in the back waist of his jeans. In the same motion, he opened the front door of the cruiser and put her inside. "Search her," he told Cameron.

The deputy did. He patted her down and then shook his head. "No other weapons."

Mandy mumbled more of those curse words. "The only reason I had that gun was because I took it from the men who kidnapped me."

Kelly prayed that was true. Actually, she hoped everything her sister had said and done wasn't part of some scheme that Kelly didn't understand or couldn't remember.

"There's an ambulance nearby," Jameson told Mandy. "We can take you to it now."

But Mandy didn't even react to that. Instead, she looked over the seat, her eyes meeting Kelly's. Kelly thought maybe she saw some relief there. Relief that didn't last long.

"The ambulance can wait," Mandy insisted. "We have to get out of here now." She tipped her head to the car behind them. "Is that your brother, Gabriel?" she asked Jameson. "The one you said you'd trust with your life?"

Jameson paused so long that for a couple of seconds Kelly didn't think he would answer. Finally, though, he nodded.

"Good. Because we might need him. But not any SAPD guys. I don't know if any of them are working for the kidnappers or not. Come on," Mandy quickly added before Jameson could argue with that. "We have to get to the baby before those men find her."

Chapter Nine

Jameson hadn't liked anything about this plan to meet Mandy, and he was liking it even less now.

"What baby?" he snapped.

"Just go. I'll explain everything once we're there. Those kidnappers will go after her."

Her. Maybe as in Boyer's daughter.

"Please," Mandy said, looking at Kelly. "If they take her, we might never find her. They could hurt her to get back at you."

Hell. That wasn't what he wanted to hear. Of course, Jameson hadn't wanted to hear that Kelly had had any part in taking the child. Because there was no way Boyer was just going to let this slide. He would put Kelly behind bars. And then there was the issue of the child. Boyer would almost certainly get custody of his own daughter—unless Jameson could come up with some kind of dirt to stop him. At the moment, though, he had more urgent problems.

"Where's the baby?" Jameson demanded.

"Just drive," Mandy insisted. "I'll tell you once we're on the highway. Make sure your brother follows us."

Oh, he would. Jameson also hoped like the devil that he wouldn't regret this. Still, if there was indeed a baby in danger, he needed to do something to save her.

"Go," Jameson told Cameron, and he made a quick call to Gabriel to let him know what was going on. He kept watch of Mandy, though, during the handful of seconds that he spoke to his brother. She didn't have a weapon and was hurt, but that didn't mean she wasn't a possible threat.

"Remember, no SAPD," Mandy said to Jameson once he was finished with the call. "It's too big of a risk to take to include them on this. If just one of them is on the take, it could cost a child her life."

Jameson wasn't immune to that threat. Especially since Kelly had indeed remembered the images of the little girl. It was a risk to go anywhere with Mandy, but he figured the biggest risk would be to stay put. After all, someone had caused that injury on Mandy's arm, and that someone could still be around.

"Take a right," Mandy instructed Cameron when he reached the end of the road.

Once the deputy had done that, Kelly made eye contact with her sister. "Start talking," Kelly said.

Mandy huffed. "I was about to tell you to do the same thing." She didn't keep her attention on her sister, though. Her gaze was firing all around, no doubt looking for those men. "Well, this is a mess. Do you know how close I came to dying?"

"Probably as close as Kelly did," Jameson countered, and he made a circling motion with his finger to prompt her to keep explaining.

Mandy opened her mouth, closed it and opened it again. "I'm not even sure where to start."

Jameson hoped this wasn't some kind of stall tactic. Just in case it was, he kept watch, as well. There wasn't much traffic on this particular road, but it only took one vehicle carrying those men to make this situation go from bad to worse.

"Start from the beginning," Jameson instructed. "And give me lots more details about where we're going and this baby that could be in harm's way."

Mandy nodded, then took a deep breath. "You mean the beginning two years ago when Kelly left?" But she didn't wait for him to confirm that. "Someone tried to kill her. That's why she ran away. And don't ask who did that because we don't know. Like I said, I thought it might be you. Guess not," she quickly added when Jameson's glare intensified.

"Where did I go?" Kelly asked. "And what happened? Why are you taking us to a baby? Whose baby is it?"

Judging from the way Mandy's eyes widened, one or more of those questions confused her. "Get on the I-35 north. Then take the second exit and turn right," Mandy said to Cameron before turning back to Kelly. "At first you went to Austin, but then there was another attack, and you moved again. I don't know where. You said it was best if no one knew."

Probably because she hadn't wanted to put her sister or anyone else in danger. But why had someone wanted her dead then? Or now, for that matter? It was too bad those memories didn't come back to her the way the other pieces had, because they desperately needed some answers.

Cameron took the ramp to the interstate, and there was plenty of traffic here, including Gabriel who was right behind them. Jameson only hoped those kidnappers hadn't managed to follow them.

"I hadn't heard from you in months," Mandy went on, talking to her sister, "and then you called me about a week ago. You asked me to meet you because you said something was wrong, that someone was following you. You thought it was August."

"August?" Kelly and Jameson repeated in unison. Jameson certainly hadn't been expecting Mandy to say that. Apparently neither had Kelly, because she made a sharp sound of surprise.

"Yeah. You told me that you believed August had turned stalker again."

Jameson looked at Kelly to see if she knew anything about this, but she only shook her head. "When did August stalk Kelly?" he asked.

"Two years ago. August had a thing for Kelly, and they even went out a few times. He was furious when he found out you'd slept with Jameson."

"That doesn't feel right," Kelly said, touching her fingers to her head. "Well, not the part about me dating August anyway. He gave me the creeps when I saw him at the sheriff's office, but he certainly didn't say a word about us going out."

"Nor has he ever said anything about it to me," Jameson added. "And I've had a lot of 'conversations' with him in the past two years."

Maybe that meant Mandy was lying. But

why would she do that—especially since it was something he could verify with August? Of course, August might not tell him the truth.

"How did August know that Kelly had slept with me?" Jameson pressed.

Mandy lifted her shoulder, then winced. A reminder that she still needed medical attention for that gunshot wound. "Beats me. But the man was always hiring PIs to help get his brother out of jail. He could have had a PI watching Kelly."

"I didn't know," Kelly whispered, and she repeated it to Jameson.

"Well, you need to be careful around him," Mandy insisted. "The man is bad news, and I wouldn't put it past him to have set those kidnappers on me. He could be responsible for the attacks on you, too."

Jameson glanced at Kelly to see how she was handling that. Not well. She hadn't exactly been steady at the start of this trip, but she was obviously learning things that were hard for her to swallow.

Things hard for Jameson to swallow, too.

Hell. That's because he was jealous. Of August, of all people. Feeling the attraction for Kelly was bad enough, and now this was eating away at him. It was also something else he had to add to a growing to-do list. But if Kelly had indeed gone out with August, Jameson needed to find out why. Because it could be connected to the nightmare that was going on right now.

Cameron took the exit, and Jameson turned away from Kelly so he could make sure there were no suspicious vehicles around them. At least the traffic was thinner here, but there were plenty of buildings.

"Later, I'm going to want to hear a whole lot more about August," Jameson clarified to Mandy. "For now, let's get back to where we're going and the baby we're going to save from these thugs."

"We're going to a safe house. Of sorts," Mandy added in a mumble. "It's something Kelly set up last week. I'm just hoping it's as safe as we need it to be. As for Boyer's daughter, Hadley came to us, begging for help…"

Jameson followed Mandy's gaze and soon saw what had snagged her attention. It was a black SUV that came out from a side road and was now right behind Gabriel. Even though the driver didn't do anything suspicious like gun the engine and try to get closer to the cruiser, it still put Jameson on edge.

"The kidnappers used a vehicle like that." Mandy's voice was suddenly a hoarse whisper. "I'd like to have that gun back now."

Jameson didn't give it to her, but like the rest

of them, they continued to watch the SUV. Apparently, Gabriel was doing the same thing because he got a text from his brother.

"Bad news?" Gabriel asked.

"Possibly," Jameson texted back.

A moment later, Mandy took her phone from her pocket, and she cursed when she looked at the screen. "Two missed calls. I'm betting this is the kidnappers. It's says Unknown Caller, but that's how their calls have been coming through."

Probably because they were using another burner cell. "You spoke to them after you escaped?"

She quickly shook her head. "No. I didn't answer. I didn't want them to hear me talking and use that to pinpoint my location."

Wise move. But Jameson very much wanted to talk to them now. He took the phone from Mandy. She reached for it as if to snatch it back from his hand, but he gave her a look that Jameson was certain could have melted ice.

"I just don't want them to find us," Mandy said. It was not only stating the obvious, but it was also an insult to him.

"I'm a Texas Ranger," he reminded her. "And I want you to stay quiet if they answer."

With that warning, Jameson hit the callback button. Even though he put it on speaker,

Kelly still moved closer to him. Until they were shoulder to shoulder.

"Didn't you learn your lesson the first time you ran, Mandy?" a man said when he answered. "You want another bullet in you?"

That meshed with what Mandy had told them, but Jameson decided to stay silent to see what the kidnapper would say. It didn't take long for the guy to continue.

"I know the cat hasn't got your tongue," the goon taunted. "And I saw you get in the cop car. I know exactly where you are."

Mandy flinched, her attention shooting right back to that SUV. Kelly didn't fare much better. She clamped her teeth over her bottom lip, but that didn't stop it from trembling.

"Yeah, you're a special kind of stupid all right," the kidnapper went on. "This isn't much of a guess, but the cop is probably listening right now. So speak up, cop. If not, I plan to open the window and just start shooting. Might not hit the cruiser or the cop behind him, but I'll sure as hell hit something."

Jameson wanted to curse, but instead he handed Kelly his own phone. "Text Gabriel and tell him what's happening," he mouthed. He didn't want his brother blindsided by shots this idiot might fire. Once she'd started that, Jameson turned his attention back to the caller.

"Why'd you take Mandy?" Jameson came out and asked him.

The guy didn't jump to answer that, but Jameson could hear him having a muffled conversation. Probably with his partner. Or rather his partners. Mandy had said two men had taken her, but that didn't mean there weren't more than that following them.

"I was following orders," the guy finally said. "Just like now. Either you and the other cop pull off the side of the road and hand over Kelly to us, or we start shooting."

"Kelly?" Jameson questioned. "I thought you were after Mandy."

"Not now that we have Kelly in our sights. And she is in our sights, cop."

Jameson wasn't sure how Kelly managed to finish the text to Gabriel because her hand was suddenly trembling as much as her mouth. She handed him back his phone.

"I can't put all of you in danger again," Kelly said. Her voice was barely audible, but Jameson heard it loud and clear.

He hoped Kelly didn't have trouble hearing him, either. "No. You're not surrendering to these nutjobs. You'll be dead within minutes if you step out of this cruiser." Just in case she had plans to jump out, Jameson took hold of her arm.

"He's right," Mandy assured her. "They want you dead."

Jameson hadn't been certain that Mandy would be willing to put herself in the path of those kidnappers, but it sounded as if she was bracing herself for a fight.

And that fight came.

"Time's up," the kidnapper snarled.

The guy ended the call, and within seconds a shot blasted through the air. That put Jameson's heart right in his throat, and he fired glances around, trying to figure out if the shooter had hit anything.

He had.

The back window of Gabriel's car had been cracked. It was bullet-resistant, but if the shots continued, eventually they'd be able to make it through.

The gunman fired again, and this time Jameson spotted the guy's hand when he stuck it out the window. It was impossible to see his face, though, because of the heavy tint on the windshield.

"Speed up," Jameson told Cameron. "Get us out of here." That way, Gabriel wouldn't be trapped between the cruiser and the SUV.

"Give me the gun, and I'll try to return fire," Mandy insisted.

Jameson couldn't say "no" fast enough. For

one thing, he didn't want the window down to make it easier for shots to get into the vehicle. There could be other gunmen stashed along the road who could do that. For another thing, he didn't want Mandy firing a shot that could hit an innocent bystander.

Cameron sped up. Behind them, Gabriel did the same. But the shooter in the SUV didn't give up. It went faster as well, and the shots continued. These bullets didn't seem to be going into Gabriel's car, either. The snake was firing random shots, trying to kill someone.

In the distance, Jameson heard the sound of sirens. Gabriel had likely called for backup for them to already be that close to the scene. That didn't mean Jameson had plans for them to slow down or stop.

"Take the next left," Mandy told Cameron.

Cameron's eyes met Jameson's in the rearview mirror, and Jameson nodded. "Where are we going?" Jameson asked her.

"That safe house." Mandy's breath was gusting now, and she had her attention pinned to the SUV. Despite the sirens, the thugs were staying right behind them and were continuing to shoot.

One of those bullets slammed into the back glass of the cruiser.

Jameson cursed, shoving Kelly down onto

the seat. "You get down, too," he told Mandy, but he didn't wait to see if she'd do that. He turned in the seat, positioning his body above Kelly and making himself ready to return fire if those shots did indeed take out the glass.

Cameron took the left turn, the tires squealing on the asphalt, and the deputy had to fight with the steering wheel to keep them from going into a skid. Beneath him, he could feel Kelly's tense muscles, and he knew she was scared. She looked up at him, their gazes connecting for just a second, but in that glimpse, Jameson also saw something else.

The determination to put an end to this.

Good. He preferred her riled than on the verge of losing it. That said, he didn't want her to do anything stupid. He'd already filled their stupid quota for the day by bringing Kelly with him and putting her in yet another life-and-death situation.

"Take another left at the stop sign," Mandy told Cameron.

Another shot smacked into the back window of the cruiser, but despite the webbed glass, Jameson was still able to see that Gabriel made the turn with them. So did the SUV. His brother stayed right behind the cruiser while the hail of gunfire continued. The only saving grace was that there wasn't much traffic on this road.

No buildings, either, so it minimized the gunman's targets.

Of course, that meant the goon continued to send shots into the cruiser.

"I see the cops," Mandy said, volleying glances all around.

So did Jameson. There were two SAPD cruisers, their blue lights flashing and the sirens blaring. They were still a good distance behind them, but at least now the SUV would be sandwiched between them.

"Hold on," Cameron warned them a split second before he reached the stop sign. The deputy slowed just enough to make the left turn and then sped up again.

Jameson watched Gabriel take the same turn. But the SUV didn't. The driver went straight through the intersection and kept going.

Getting away.

"You want me to go after him?" Cameron asked.

It was tempting, especially since these goons had endangered so many people, but Kelly and Mandy had already had enough risks for the day. For a lifetime, really.

"No. Keep going," Jameson answered. Behind them, the SAPD cops went in pursuit of the SUV. Good. Maybe they'd catch the SOBs.

Kelly got up from the seat, glancing back at

the messed-up glass before turning to her sister. "How far is this safe house?"

"Not far." Mandy paused. Stared at her. "You really don't remember?"

"No. How far?" Kelly repeated.

Mandy looked at the road, which was leading them to a rural area. In fact, there were no visible houses, just pastures. "About two miles. But we need to keep watch to make sure those men aren't following us."

Jameson was already doing that. There was no one behind Gabriel, and they hadn't yet passed any immediate side roads, where a gunman could park and wait. That was about to change, though.

"Take a right at the stop sign just ahead," Mandy instructed Cameron. Unlike Jameson, she kept her attention nailed to Kelly while Cameron took the turn. "Kelly, you're sure you want to go here?"

That spiked Jameson's concern a significant notch. "Why wouldn't she?" he snapped. "You said we needed to go here to make sure the men didn't get to the baby."

Mandy nodded without even looking at him. "Are you sure?"

"If it can save a child, then yes, I'm sure," Kelly said. But she didn't sound certain at all. Neither was Jameson.

There was also plenty of wariness in Cameron's eyes when he looked back at Jameson, silently asking him what to do.

Jameson leaned forward and got right in Mandy's face. "If this is a trap, you'll pay and pay hard. Understand?"

"No trap," she assured him in a ragged whisper. "Pull into the driveway just ahead," she added to Cameron.

Jameson got his gun ready again, and he handed Kelly the weapon he'd taken from Mandy. He prayed she didn't have to use it, but he needed her to be ready for anything.

"Anything" definitely wasn't what Jameson had expected.

The moment that Cameron turned into the driveway, Jameson saw the one-story white house. Not a fortress or a trap. It looked like, well, a home. There was a picket fence surrounding the yard, which was dotted with shrubs and flowers. And the place wasn't empty. There was a blond-haired woman sitting on the porch in a rocking chair.

The woman wasn't alone. Beside her on the porch was a little girl. A toddler. She was wearing pink shorts and a white top, and the vehicles got both their attention. The woman stood, scooping up the little girl, her motions jerky and fast as if she was ready to bolt with her. She might have done just that, too, but she stopped when Mandy stepped from the cruiser.

Even though Jameson was about ten yards from the woman, he saw the relief on her face. It didn't last, though, because she spotted the blood on Mandy's sleeve.

"You're hurt," the woman called out. "What happened? Do we need to leave? Has there been more trouble?"

Mandy waved it off and went closer. "Kelly's with me." She added something else to the woman, something that Jameson couldn't hear.

That put him on full alert, and he stepped from the cruiser in case Mandy had just given this woman the order to attack. But no attack. The woman carried the baby off the porch and stood her in the yard. The little girl grinned and toddled her way toward Mandy. The kid obviously wasn't very good at walking, because she teetered a few times as if she might fall.

Jameson was so focused on what was playing out in front of him that he didn't notice Kelly opening the door until it was too late. She got out, and since she was on the other side of the car, he couldn't get to her before she started going closer to the house.

As the woman had done with Mandy, she smiled at Kelly. So did the little girl. The baby immediately changed directions, no longer headed toward Mandy but straight to Kelly.

Jameson hurried to them, his gaze slashing all around in case they were about to be ambushed. But there didn't seem to be a threat. The woman certainly didn't seem alarmed.

When Kelly reached the baby, the little girl outstretched her arms for Kelly to pick her up. And Jameson had no trouble hearing the one word that the child babbled.

"Mama."

Chapter Ten

Mama?

Kelly glanced at her sister to see if she had an explanation, but Mandy kept walking. "We shouldn't be out here," Mandy finally said when she reached the porch. "Bring Gracelyn inside with you."

Gracelyn. That apparently was the child's name. And her sister was right. They shouldn't be out there. Jameson must have thought so, too, because he scooped up the little girl, shifting her to his hip, and he hooked his arm around Kelly to get her moving. Gabriel, Cameron and Susan, the other deputy, were right behind them.

"Mama," the little girl repeated, and she tried to wiggle out of Jameson's arms to get to Kelly.

Kelly knew what all of this meant. She'd been the one to raise Boyer's daughter. She'd been the child's mother.

She tucked Mandy's gun in the back of her

jeans and took Gracelyn from Jameson when the girl just kept squirming. The child immediately kissed Kelly's cheek. It was as if someone had warmed her from head to toe, and Kelly was positive what she was feeling was love. A mother's love.

"Pat, pat," Gracelyn said.

"She learned to play patty-cake," the woman on the porch supplied. Kelly had no idea who she was, but the moment they reached her, she pulled Kelly into a short hug. "I'm glad you made it back." Her attention drifted to Kelly's bandage. "Are you okay?"

"No." Kelly could say that with complete certainty. Every inch of her was still spinning from the adrenaline, and she was getting more of those fragments of memories.

Fragments that didn't make sense.

"Pat, pat," Gracelyn repeated.

Jameson gave the little girl a long glance. Frowned. And he kept them moving. Once they were all inside, he shut the door and locked it.

"First things first," Jameson said. "Mandy, make sure you don't have a tracking device on you."

She groaned and looked ready to curse, but she stopped when her gaze landed on Gracelyn. Mandy began to look over her clothes and shoes. Kelly helped, too. Balancing the baby on her hip, she checked Mandy's hair and the back of her shirt.

"I don't see anything," Kelly relayed to Jameson when she'd finished.

"Want to tell me what the heck is going on?" Gabriel growled. "And who she is?" He tipped his head to the woman before going to the window to keep watch. The two deputies went to other windows to do the same.

The sheriff was obviously riled, maybe about this latest attack, maybe because they'd been brought here with such little information. But despite that, things suddenly started to feel, well, right. It must have felt right for Gracelyn, too, because she dropped her head onto Kelly's shoulder as if it belonged there.

"This is Erica Welker," Mandy said, looking at Kelly. Mandy went to the adjacent kitchen and came back with a first-aid kit.

The name meant nothing to her, and Erica must have seen the surprise on Kelly's face, because she made a slight gasp. "What's wrong?"

Kelly decided to keep the answer short, especially since Mandy had so much explaining to do. "I have amnesia and don't remember a lot of things. I'm sorry, but I don't know who you are."

Erica stood there, her mouth not open exactly, but she did have a gobsmacked expression on her face. "But you remember Gracelyn?"

"I have some memories of her." Kelly shifted her attention back to her sister, who was now in the process of ripping off her shirtsleeve, no doubt so she could examine her wound. Kelly didn't come out and ask Mandy to start talking. However, Jameson's and Gabriel's glares must have prompted her sister to do that.

Mandy looked at Erica. "Could you take Gracelyn to her room to play?"

Erica volleyed uneasy glances at all of them before she nodded and took the little girl. Gracelyn started to protest, babbling "Mama," but she stopped when Erica said she would read to her. Kelly kept her eyes on them as they walked away, and the moment Gracelyn was out of sight, she felt the loss. Or something. It caused her chest to tighten when she could no longer see the child.

"FYI, there's a whole lot about what I'm going to say that none of you will like," Mandy began. When she started to clean away the blood from her arm, Kelly went to her and took over the task. It appeared the wound was shallow, but it was still bleeding.

"I haven't liked much of anything since this whole mess started," Jameson assured her. "But I want to hear it anyway."

Mandy took a deep breath. "I've already told you that Kelly called me about a week ago. She said she was worried that someone, maybe August, was stalking her. She asked me to help her protect Gracelyn."

"Why would August want to harm a kid?" Jameson snapped.

"Kelly thought he might try to take her to use her for leverage in something he was planning. Maybe like a last-ditch effort to get his brother out of jail. I didn't think August would do anything like that," Mandy quickly added, "but then someone did try to kidnap Kelly and Gracelyn. They escaped, and Kelly brought Gracelyn and Erica here."

"Erica's a nanny?" Kelly asked.

Mandy nodded. "She used to be a PI, though. She worked for us when we still had the agency."

So more of a bodyguard than a mere nanny. Of course, that didn't surprise Kelly that they would need that. After all, she'd probably been in hiding with the child since she was born, and she probably trusted Erica.

"Anyway," Mandy went on, "we were here for a few days, and nothing happened. No more attacks. So I decided to go back to my place and get some supplies. That's when those two thugs kidnapped me. They were going to hold me and force Kelly to do whatever it was they wanted her to do."

"Kill Jameson," Kelly quickly provided. "I had a note telling me to do that. But why Jameson?"

Mandy huffed and then winced when Kelly dabbed the wound with antiseptic. "Again, I'm sure you think it's August trying to get back at the Becketts for putting his brother in jail. But I believe Boyer's behind what's happening."

"You mean because of his daughter," Kelly said under her breath.

"No. Because he's dirty. August thinks so, too, because he asked us to look into some money laundering rumors. Rumors that Boyer was stealing federally confiscated funds and then funneling them into his own private offshore bank account."

Now it was Jameson who huffed. "Why the hell would August care a rat about Boyer doing something like that?"

"August thought Boyer was going to set him up for it," Mandy answered without hesitation. "You must know that Boyer was investigating August?"

They did know that because Boyer had told them at the sheriff's office. Still, there was something that didn't make sense. "Did we find anything to incriminate either Boyer or August?" Kelly asked.

"Yeah." And that's all Mandy said for several long moments. "You apparently found a money trail, and when this recent trouble started, you were trying to figure out who owned the account because it seemed to be connected to the money laundering that August thought Boyer was doing."

Well, that would certainly make someone want to stop her. But it made Kelly wonder— how had August or Boyer known about her investigation into that money trail? Had someone tipped them off?

Jameson cursed. "You should have gone to the cops with this." He aimed that snarl at Kelly.

And she deserved it. But Kelly knew why she hadn't done that, why it was critical for her to find something that would put Boyer behind bars.

"I didn't go to the cops because I couldn't," Kelly reminded him. "Because I'd stolen Boyer's daughter."

Since Kelly still had her fingers on her sister's arm, she felt Mandy's muscles go stiff. Mandy looked up at her, and Kelly didn't understand what she was seeing in her sister's eyes.

"You'll want to sit down for this," Mandy

said before shifting her attention to Jameson. "You, too."

Jameson cursed again. "I'm not sitting down. Just tell us..." His words trailed off, and he glanced in the direction of where they'd last seen Erica and the baby. "How old is Gracelyn?"

Mandy's arm muscles tightened even more, and she pulled Kelly into the chair next to her. "She's fourteen months."

The room went still and silent. But that didn't apply to what was going on inside Kelly. Or Jameson, for that matter. He groaned. It was hoarse and raw and came deep from within his chest.

"She's not Boyer's daughter," Jameson somehow managed to say. He took the words right out of Kelly's mouth, and she had no trouble taking this one step further. Gracelyn wasn't Boyer's.

That's when Kelly knew Gracelyn was her and Jameson's child.

Jameson turned a very nasty glare in Kelly's direction, and it had a dangerous edge to it. He looked ready to explode. Kelly wanted to tell him that she hadn't remembered giving birth to the child, much less keeping her from him, but the words froze in her throat.

Because she did remember.

It all came flooding back. The night she'd landed in bed with Jameson. Running and hiding after someone had attacked her. There were even bits and pieces of the pregnancy. What wasn't a bit or piece, though, was what she felt for her daughter. She loved her more than life itself.

"Why?" Jameson said, and his tone matched that tight, lethal expression on his face.

"Someone was trying to kill her," Mandy supplied.

That wouldn't be enough to appease Jameson. No. Because he was a Ranger, and he would have expected her to go to him instead of running. Except she'd just stolen that file and hadn't even known if she could trust him.

"I need to see Gracelyn," Kelly insisted.

Jameson clearly didn't like that, but Kelly didn't take the time to say anything else. Everything inside her was urging her to get to her baby. To make sure she was okay. Later, she could hash things out with Jameson.

And it wouldn't be pretty.

Kelly hurried to the room where she'd seen Erica take the baby, and she threw open the door. Erica was sitting on the floor, Gracelyn in her lap, but the little girl had fallen asleep.

"She was tired from playing outside," Erica mouthed. She brushed a kiss on Gracelyn's head, and then did a double take of Kelly when she looked at her. "What's wrong? Did those kidnappers find us?"

Heavens, she hoped not. Now that she knew this precious baby was hers, Kelly had to do everything to protect her.

She went closer, sitting down on the bed next to Erica, and the nanny stood, easing Gracelyn into her arms. Kelly felt that same punch of love that she'd felt in the yard.

"Should I give you some time alone?" Erica asked.

The nanny didn't mean that offer for only Kelly and Gracelyn. That's because Jameson was in the doorway. He had anchored his hands on the jamb as if holding himself back.

"Yes, please," Kelly answered. Erica didn't jump to leave. She glanced at them, maybe trying to make sure it was safe to leave them alone with this cowboy cop. "It's okay," she added to Erica. "Jameson is Gracelyn's father."

The words hadn't stuck in her throat, and even though she'd just spelled out what Jameson already knew, he flinched a little. He stepped to the side to let Erica out, and then he came to them, sitting on the bed next to her.

"I should have told you," Kelly volunteered. "And there's nothing I can say to make this right. 'I'm sorry' certainly isn't going to do it."

A sound left his mouth. Almost a laugh, but it definitely wasn't from humor. He didn't say anything. Jameson just sat there, staring at their daughter.

Their daughter.

Kelly wondered how long it was going to take for that to sink in. Not just for Jameson, but also for her.

She studied Gracelyn's face and saw some parts of herself there. The shape of her mouth and eyes. But the coloring was all Jameson. Dark hair and olive skin. Kelly wondered why she hadn't noticed it the moment she laid eyes on the child.

"Do you doubt she's yours?" Kelly asked.

"No." Jameson didn't hesitate for even a second.

Kelly wasn't sure if that was good or bad. On the one hand, if Jameson didn't believe this was his child, he could just walk away and hand over their protective custody to someone else. But now that he knew Gracelyn was his, Kelly figured that meant he was going to work extra hard to make sure nothing bad happened to her.

He groaned, scrubbed his hand over his face and then turned to her. "I want to hate you for this."

She mentally repeated each word. "I hate myself for it."

"That doesn't make us even. It doesn't make it right."

Kelly was in total agreement with that. This was a mess, and it was all her own doing. "I must have thought I couldn't trust you."

That wasn't a good thing to say. It put more of that angry fire in Jameson's eyes. "You could have, but instead you kept her from me for over a year." He groaned again, and she could see this was eating away at him.

It was eating away at her, too. She touched her fingers to his arm, but he only jerked away from her. "I'm not going to give you a free pass on this," he said like a warning. "I'm not going to let you cut me out of her life again."

That stung as much as if he'd slapped her. Not just the words, but the raw anger in his voice. Anger that she'd need to face. It didn't matter that she only had pieces of her memories; she somehow had to make this right. And that was a reminder that making things right started with Gracelyn's safety.

"We can't stay here," Kelly said.

"No," he agreed. "I need to get started on that. But just know that this conversation isn't over."

She hadn't thought for a moment that it was. As if it were the most natural thing in the world, Jameson brushed a kiss on the baby's forehead, and he stood. However, he'd barely made it a step when Gabriel appeared in the doorway. The sheriff was still scowling, and he had his phone pressed to his ear. He motioned for Jameson to follow him.

Kelly's stomach sank, because she figured this wasn't good news. She got up, cradling the baby in her arms so she could follow him. By the time she made it back to the living room, Gabriel had finished his phone conversation and had turned to Jameson.

"That was SAPD," Gabriel said. "Those men in the SUV got away."

It felt as if someone had punched her, and it caused Kelly's head to throb even more. Not good. It was already too hard to think, and the pain was only making it worse.

Mandy bit off some of the profanity she was mumbling. "How did that happen?" she asked Gabriel.

"The men turned on a side road and ditched the SUV. The cops believe they had another vehicle stashed there and used it to escape." Gabriel paused, stared at her. "Any chance those men know where this place is?"

"No," her sister answered. "If they'd known the location, they would have already come here. For the baby," Mandy added in a whisper.

Yes, because if they had Gracelyn, then they knew Kelly would do anything to get her back.

Mandy's attention went to the baby for a moment. "The only way for those goons to find this place would be by putting a tracking device on me, and you've already searched me."

The moment her sister finished saying that, Jameson cursed, and he yanked the phone from his pocket. Not his phone but the one Mandy had stolen from the kidnappers. He immediately started taking it apart.

Oh, God. Kelly prayed there was nothing to find.

"Check the gun, too," Jameson said, aiming a glance at Kelly.

That spiked her heart rate even more, and since Kelly didn't want to handle the gun while she was holding the baby, she turned so that Gabriel could take it from the back of her jeans. Like Jameson, he immediately started to inspect it. But his inspection didn't last long because Jameson dumped the pieces of the phone onto the coffee table.

Kelly saw it then. The white disk that was about the size of a quarter. Even though she still didn't have many memories of being a PI, she knew exactly what it was. And what it meant. The kidnappers had planted it there and intentionally let Mandy take it so she would lead them here to the baby.

"We have to leave now," Jameson insisted. He snapped toward the deputies. "Pull the cruisers right up to the porch."

That sent Erica and Mandy scurrying, and Kelly realized they were gathering up the baby's things. Obviously, they had been prepared for something like this. But Kelly certainly wasn't. The other attacks had terrified her, but this was a whole new level of terror.

Because Gracelyn could be hurt.

Cameron drew his gun, opened the door, but just as quickly, he slammed it shut. "Are you expecting company?" he asked Mandy.

Mandy shook her head, and she hurried to the window along with Gabriel and Jameson. Kelly could tell from their body language that this wasn't good.

The gunmen had found them.

Chapter Eleven

They had already dodged bullets from Mandy's kidnappers, but Jameson should have known it wasn't over. He'd let the news of the baby—*his* baby—distract him, and that could turn out to be a fatal mistake.

He needed to push aside that baby news and the emotions that came with it and focus on getting them out of this.

"Go to the back door," Jameson told Susan. "Make sure it's locked and that these guys don't try to sneak up on us." There weren't any houses back there. Not that Jameson had seen anyway, but it was possible there were trees and shrubs that one of these hired guns could use.

"Check all the windows. Look for any vulnerable points of attack," Gabriel added to Cameron, and the deputies hurried off to do those tasks.

"Is there a bathroom without windows?" Jameson asked Mandy.

She nodded. "There's one just off the hall."

Good. That was a start, though it wasn't ideal since bullets could go through walls and still reach them. "Take Erica and Gracelyn there, now," he told Kelly.

Jameson could see the stark fear in Kelly's eyes, but he couldn't assure her that this was going to turn out well. It could end up in a gunfight, though that wasn't what Jameson wanted. Not with his daughter in the house.

Gabriel took out his phone, no doubt to call for backup, and while Jameson kept watch, he quickly reassembled the phone Mandy had taken. Right now, it was the only way he had to communicate with these snakes other than opening the door and going out there to face them down.

"One of them is getting out of the first SUV," Gabriel relayed.

Yeah, Jameson saw the gun. He got out from the driver's side, which meant the SUV was in between him and them. Jameson doubted that was a coincidence. The guy was using it for cover, and he was no doubt armed to the hilt.

Kelly's gaze connected with his as she started moving. "Be careful," she said, but she frowned as if that weren't nearly enough.

She was right. Words alone weren't going to fix this, or their personal situation for that matter, but if the thugs heard backup arriving, they might run again. Of course, they might be a good fifteen or twenty minutes from that happening.

Jameson waited until Erica, Gracelyn and Kelly had gone into the bathroom, and he shot a look at Mandy to prompt her to go, too. "I'm staying," she insisted. "But I need a gun."

He debated it, because Jameson still had a strange feeling about her, but he finally handed her the gun she'd taken from the kidnappers. Maybe she wouldn't have to use it.

Jameson moved back into position at the window, and while keeping watch, he pressed the button to call the kidnappers. He wasn't certain they would answer, but they did on the first ring. He put the call on speaker so that Gabriel would be able to hear.

"You probably thought you'd gotten away," a man immediately growled. "Now it's time to pay."

Jameson didn't even bother to address that threat. "Backup is on the way."

"We figured it was. That's why this'll have to be fast. Give us Kelly, and the kid and everybody else will be okay."

Even if Jameson had believed that, he wouldn't have handed over Kelly. But he soon realized Kelly might have a different notion about that. He heard the movement behind him and saw that Kelly was in the doorway of the bathroom. She no longer had Gracelyn in her arms, but she'd clearly heard what the thug had said.

"Why do you want me?" she demanded, and she charged forward toward Jameson and the phone.

"You know why," the man answered. "So just step outside, and there won't be a shot fired. You gotta know that's best for the kid and everybody else in the house. That includes your cop boyfriend."

The hired gun had done his homework. Or else his boss had filled him in. It made Jameson wonder if these thugs knew that Gracelyn was his daughter. Or maybe they believed she was Boyer's, just as Jameson had before Mandy dropped the bombshell.

Jameson gave Kelly the meanest scowl he could manage, and he motioned for her to go back in the bathroom. "If you go out there, they'll kill you and then try to shoot everyone in this house. They aren't going to leave witnesses."

"Now, now," the thug taunted, but he didn't deny it. He couldn't. The guy wasn't wearing a mask, and even though Jameson hadn't gotten a good look at his face, there was no way these goons would want to leave alive four officers and a PI.

Jameson kept the scowl on Kelly until she huffed and went back to the bathroom. Once she was inside, he returned his full attention to the caller.

"I don't know what you're being paid," Jameson told him, "but it's not nearly enough. Because you're going to die if you stay here."

He figured that would prompt the guy to give him another taunt. It didn't. The man lifted his hand over the hood of the SUV and pointed his gun at the house.

And he fired.

The shot slammed into the house, right next to the window where Jameson was standing. It wasn't the only shot, either. Several more came, and one of them crashed through the window and sent glass spewing over the room.

"There's one in the backyard!" Susan called out.

Hell. That wasn't what Jameson wanted to hear. Neither did Gabriel, because he cursed.

"If you have a shot, take it," Gabriel shouted back. "Just don't let him get in the house."

Jameson hit the end call button so the goons wouldn't be able to hear what they were saying. There were more shots, not coming from the guy by the SUV this time. Jameson quickly realized they also weren't coming from the back. They had slammed into the side of the house.

"I got a shooter," Cameron let them know.

That caused the skin to crawl on the back of his neck, and Jameson's thoughts jerked to a really bad place. If these thugs had the house surrounded, they could keep shooting until they ripped it apart, and backup might not arrive in time to stop them.

Gabriel didn't repeat his warning to Cameron about not letting the guy in the house. His brother knocked out the glass on the side window where he was positioned, and he started shooting.

Jameson did the same.

That sent the guy behind the SUV dropping out of sight, but the gunfire continued on the side of the house. Worse, he heard shots at the back, too. "See if Susan or Cameron need help," Jameson told Mandy. "But stay close to the bathroom door."

He didn't need to spell out why he wanted her to do that, but if these thugs did make it inside, Jameson wanted someone standing guard to stop them from getting to Gracelyn and Kelly.

"There's one at your three o'clock," Gabriel said.

Because of his angle, Jameson didn't spot the guy at first, but then he saw him crawling toward the picket fence. Jameson took aim and put two bullets in him. The guy quit crawling. Whether he was dead or not was anyone's guess, but maybe he was at least out of commission.

"How much ammo do you have?" Jameson asked his brother.

"A lot. So do Cameron and Susan. You?"

"Plenty." He'd stocked up before they'd left to go find Mandy. "I'm thinking of trying to shoot out the SUV engine. They might get worried if they realize I can disable their ride. It could cause them to run."

Of course, part of him didn't want them to run. Jameson wanted to face them down and arrest the SOBs. But that was too big of a risk to take with the others in the house.

"Go for it," Gabriel agreed. "As long as you're shooting at the engine, it might keep thug number one pinned down."

That was a good side benefit. An even better one would be if he managed to shoot the idiot in the head.

Jameson aimed his gun and started firing. His shot slammed into the SUV's engine, and it got the reaction he wanted. The engine started to spew steam, which meant he'd hit the radiator. He caught a glimpse of thug number one scrambling to get back inside. He drove off, but it wouldn't get far. Nor did the second SUV go with him. It stayed put, making Jameson wonder if the hired guns who'd been inside were now the ones at the sides and back of the house.

More shots blasted through the air, all coming from the back of the house, and then Jameson heard a sound that he definitely didn't want to hear.

Breaking glass.

Not from the back or from where Cameron was, either. No. This had come from the other side. He didn't know the layout of the house, but it sounded as if it'd come from the window in the room next to the bathroom.

"Go!" Gabriel ordered him.

But Jameson had already started running. However, before he even made it to the hall, there was a different sound. A welcome one. Sirens. That meant backup had arrived. It would probably send the men outside running, but it was the one inside who was the immediate threat. He could start shooting before the backup officers even got out of their vehicles.

The bathroom door was shut, thank God, and it was hopefully locked, but the door adjacent to it was slightly ajar. With his gun ready, Jameson peered around the corner.

No gunman. However, he did see the broken glass on the floor. That twisted his gut into a knot.

Jameson couldn't risk the idiot firing into the bathroom, so he couldn't wait to see what this guy was planning. He dragged in a deep breath and gave the door a hard kick.

He got lucky.

Because the door smacked right into the thug who'd just started to move toward him. The guy froze, and that gave Jameson enough time to take aim at him.

"Move," Jameson warned him, "and you're a dead man."

KELLY HAD SO many emotions running through her that it felt as if there were a F5 tornado in her head. Too bad, because she needed to think. Needed to figure out what was happening so she could stop it.

It was almost a cliché, but this was one of the worst and best times of her life. She had her baby, a baby she hadn't even remembered existed, and that was an incredible feeling. On the other side of the coin, though, her precious little girl was in danger.

"Pat, pat," Gracelyn said, drawing Kelly's attention back to her. Not that it had strayed far. She hadn't let her baby out of her sight on the trip from the house to the sheriff's office.

And wouldn't.

But this wasn't an ideal situation for any of them. Gracelyn was on a quilt in the break room at the back of the building. It would be night soon, and she didn't like the idea of her little girl having to sleep here. Thankfully, Gracelyn didn't seem to mind and was having fun alternating her play sessions among Erica, Mandy and Kelly.

Jameson, too.

He was working the investigation from Gabriel's office, but he kept popping in every ten minutes or so. Each time he came in, he zoomed right in on Gracelyn and once had even taken her picture with his phone. The glances he spared Kelly weren't exactly of a friendly nature, and she couldn't blame him. He would probably never forgive her for this.

After she finished off another cup of coffee, Mandy sank down on the floor next to them, and Kelly didn't miss her sister wincing when her arm brushed against the sofa.

"The doctor left you some pain meds," Kelly reminded her.

He'd done that when he had come to the sheriff's office to stitch up Mandy and examine both Kelly and the baby. Gracelyn didn't have a bruise or scratch on her. That was something, at least. If she'd been hurt in all of this, Kelly wouldn't have been able to stomach it.

"The doc left you some pain meds, too," Mandy pointed out just as quickly.

He had. But Kelly shook her head. "They might make me woozy."

"Ditto," Mandy agreed. "I'm thinking this isn't a good time to be out of it."

No. They might have to move again at a moment's notice. The sheriff's office was safe. Probably. But it was only temporary.

"Maybe Jameson will get some info from the gunman he captured," Erica suggested. Despite the serious conversation, the nanny smiled at Gracelyn when she babbled something.

Kelly made a sound of agreement to Erica's comment. She was hoping that would happen, too, but so far the yet-to-be-identified man wasn't giving them much. Like his comrade, McGill, who was still in custody. Both men had lawyered up. At least the most recent captive wasn't claiming that Kelly was the one behind this.

"FYI, I didn't know about Gracelyn until long after she was born," Mandy said a moment later.

Kelly tried to work through the clutter in her head to figure out why she wouldn't have told her. "Maybe I thought it would put you in danger if you knew."

Mandy shrugged, winced again. "If you'd told me sooner, though, I could have helped you. Like with that file from Jameson's office, for instance. As soon as you got your hands on it, you didn't tell me squat about what any of the notes and such meant to you. But that file could be the reason these snakes are after all of us now."

That immediately troubled Kelly. Why wouldn't she have shared that with Mandy? They were business partners. Fellow PIs. Again, it was possible she realized the info was lethal and she hadn't wanted to involve Mandy. For all the good it'd done. Obviously, Mandy had gotten involved when those kidnappers took her.

"I feel like an idiot," Mandy continued, groaning softly. "I should have known it was too easy for me to steal that phone and gun. Those men wanted me to lead them straight to you and Gracelyn. And that's exactly what I did."

"You didn't know." Kelly slipped her hand over her sister's.

But they certainly knew now, and it was proof of just how far these monsters would go to get to her.

She was about to ask if Mandy could fill her in on the months she'd been hiding. Those after Gracelyn had been born. But before she could say anything, Jameson opened the door. As with his other visits, he looked at Gracelyn first. Smiled. Gracelyn returned the smile and babbled something again.

"Is she okay?" Jameson asked.

Kelly nodded, and Gracelyn got up and started toddling toward her. She clearly hadn't been walking that long because she was still a little unsteady, but Jameson met her part of the way, and he scooped her up in his arms.

"I'm working on a place for us to go," Jameson explained to them. "It shouldn't be much longer."

He didn't add any other details, and Kelly didn't ask. She trusted that Jameson would do what was best. Unfortunately, even his best might not be enough.

"Pat, pat," Gracelyn said, clearly wanting him to play the game.

Jameson glanced around as if trying to figure out what to do, but his hesitation didn't last long. He sank down on the sofa, positioning Gracelyn so she was facing him, and he did something that stunned Kelly.

He played patty-cake.

It was a sight that got Mandy's and Erica's

attention, too. A hot cowboy with a baby on his lap. Kelly hadn't even known he knew how to play patty-cake. The sight of them warmed her. And put a lump in her throat.

When he finished two rounds of the game, Jameson kissed Gracelyn's cheek and sat her back on the quilt. In the same motion, he looked at Kelly. "We need to talk. In Gabriel's office," he added.

Kelly didn't like the sound of that. This was either bad news about the investigation or Jameson was ready to rake her over the coals for keeping Gracelyn from him.

She gave Gracelyn a kiss, too, before she followed Jameson out of the room and to Gabriel's office just up the hall. Kelly expected to find other cops there, but it was empty. Jameson had obviously been working, though, because there was a laptop on the desk, which was cluttered with open files and paper.

"When did you learn to play patty-cake?" she asked at the same moment that Jameson said, "The second gunman is Weldon Rosa. His name might sound familiar to you because he was a former client of yours."

Both stopped, maybe surprised by what the other had said. Kelly was certainly surprised anyway. She shook her head. "I don't recognize him."

"Maybe because you never actually met him." Jameson blew out a long breath and scrubbed his hand over the back of his neck. "According to your computer records, you had an appointment scheduled with him around the time you disappeared. It's possible you never showed for that appointment."

"Or maybe he's the reason I went on the run. Mandy did say someone had tried to kill me."

He nodded and made a sound that caused her to think he'd already come to that conclusion. "I learned to play patty-cake with Cameron's nephew. Cameron lives on the ranch with him, and he brings him to my house sometimes."

Kelly couldn't help it. She smiled at the thought of that. It didn't last. And just as quickly, she felt the tears burning her eyes. Tears that she cursed.

"I like kids," he added. "I always wanted one or two of my own."

She hadn't known that about him. Of course, they hadn't dated that long before things had gone to Hades in a handbasket. Kelly could blame herself for that.

"I'm so sorry," she said. "Not just about Gracelyn—"

"Stop," he snapped. His tone was as lethal as those glares he'd been giving her. But like her smile, the glare didn't last, either. Maybe because she hadn't been successful in fighting back those blasted tears.

Jameson cursed under his breath, touched her arm. "It's a rough time for all of us." The corner of his mouth lifted a little. Almost a smile. "That's the mother of all understatements."

That helped with the tears. Some. But she really did want him to know how sorry she was.

"How can I make this right?" she asked.

His eyes came to hers, and he stared at her as if waiting for something. Maybe for the answer to come to him. Judging from the way he bunched up his forehead, it wasn't coming. Maybe because there was no way for her to fix things between them.

She wiped away a tear that made it onto her cheek. But Jameson wiped away the second one. His touch was a surprise. A welcome one. His fingers were warm on her skin. Strange that a simple touch from Jameson could suddenly make her feel a whole lot better.

Kelly expected him to move away. That's what he usually did whenever they got close. But he didn't. On a heavy sigh, Jameson slipped his arm around her waist and inched her to him. The touch had been a drop in the bucket compared to having her body against his again. There was more warmth. The attraction.

And memories.

More of those fragments came. Of another time he'd held her. Also when he'd kissed her.

She stood there, so close to him, and her body picked up the rhythm of his breathing. Her pulse was already thick and throbbing, and it only got worse when he pulled back just a fraction. That's because Kelly thought this was all going to end.

It didn't.

He studied her, easing her hair from her face. She could see the debate in his eyes, and he was trying to make himself put an end to this. Because she was a complication that he didn't want or need. He cursed again, and that was the only warning Kelly got before his mouth came to hers.

There. That's what she wanted. And she didn't need her full memory back to know that. The kiss suddenly made the heat ripple through her. It didn't stay a ripple, either. When Jameson kept kissing her, her body responded. So did his. She could feel him against the zipper of her jeans.

Kelly slipped her arms around his neck, pulling him down to her. Not that they could get any closer, but Jameson didn't fight it. In fact, he added to the complication by turning her and pressing her back against the wall. She hadn't thought they could get any closer, but Kelly had been wrong.

The kiss didn't stop, and Jameson deepened it when he took hold of the back of her neck. The fire was already too hot, but that created an urgency. A bad one. Because there was only one fix for it.

A fix they couldn't have.

Even if her body was suggesting otherwise.

Jameson finally stepped back, probably because he needed air. Time to regroup, too. And she saw the moment he realized just what a stupid mistake this was. Not only had it caused them to lose focus, but this intimacy also added to the complications. They had enough of those without acting on the attraction.

Dragging in some breaths and cursing himself, Jameson stepped back even farther from her. Not a second too soon, either. Because Gabriel appeared in the doorway. He opened his mouth and looked at them. As if he knew exactly what had happened between them, he shook his head.

"We have a visitor," Gabriel said.

"Yeah, and you need to see me," someone added.

August.

Despite the scowl Gabriel gave him, August came to the door, as well. His mouth tightened when his attention landed on them. Like Gabriel, he seemed to know they'd just kissed. Apparently, Jameson and she looked guilty as sin.

"I'm glad you're here," Jameson said to August. "I have some questions for you."

August's eyes went wide. "What are you talking about?" But he quickly waved that off. "Save your allegations and slander for later. Right now, you have a much bigger problem on your hands."

It took Kelly a moment to realize that August was talking to her. "What do you mean?"

"I mean Boyer." August huffed. "Now he's claiming that I helped you steal his daughter. And he's headed over here with some kind of paperwork. My lawyers think it might be arrest warrants for both of us."

Chapter Twelve

Jameson didn't need a complication like this. Not with so many other things going on. And especially since he hadn't found any proof that Kelly had taken Boyer's child. Those baby memories she'd had were of their own child.

Kelly shook her head, her gaze slashing to Jameson's. "I can't go with Boyer," she insisted. "You can't let him take me."

Agreed. If it was an arrest warrant, though, Jameson wasn't sure how to handle it. His first instinct was to get both Kelly and Gracelyn out of there, but that could be what Boyer or the goon behind the attacks wanted them to do. That way, they'd have another chance to kill Kelly.

But staying put meant Jameson would somehow have to stall the agent. Or defy a court order. He would do either or both. In fact, he'd do whatever it took to keep them safe, but it could land him in jail, too. No way could he let that happen.

Gabriel was right behind August, and his brother had obviously heard the conversation. That was no doubt what had put the fresh troubled look on his face. "I'll talk to Boyer," Gabriel offered.

"Yes, and tell him to back off," August snapped. "This witch hunt of his is getting old."

Probably not in Boyer's mind. Now that Jameson was a father, he understood why the agent couldn't let go of the search for his child. Jameson wouldn't have given up, either, and he would have gone after anyone who could give him answers. Unfortunately, they couldn't give that to Boyer.

But maybe August could.

"Talk to me about you stalking Kelly," Jameson threw out there while he stared at the man.

August pulled back his shoulders. Obviously, Jameson had managed to shock him, and August shifted his attention to Kelly. "You told him that? Because it's not true. You're mixing up the memories."

"Mandy told me," Kelly quietly added.

Now August's mouth tightened. "Your sister is wrong. *You* were wrong. I had feelings for you once, and you misinterpreted my concern as stalking."

Jameson groaned. "That sounds like something a stalker would say."

August's glare was scalpel-sharp. "I was worried about Kelly. Mandy, too. Obviously, I was right to feel that way, because someone wants them dead."

Not *them*.

Only Kelly.

Those gunmen had intentionally let Mandy go. Of course, that didn't mean they wouldn't come after her later, but they'd had ample opportunity to kill her and they hadn't.

Gabriel held up his phone, letting Jameson know he had a call coming in, and he stepped away, heading back to the squad room. Probably so he would be able to stop Boyer when the agent arrived. His brother likely wouldn't be able to stop him for long, though, and that's why they needed to get rid of August so Jameson could talk to Kelly about their limited options of dealing with this.

"Mandy said we dated once or twice," Kelly relayed to August. There was some disgust in her voice.

Disgust that Jameson felt, and he knew why. It was jealousy, plain and simple. Yeah, that kiss had thrown off his perspective. So had learning about Gracelyn. And it wasn't a good time to lose his objectivity.

"We dated, briefly. It didn't work out between us." He paused. "You wanted information from me, and I'm pretty sure that's the only reason you agreed to go out with me. Heck, you never even let me kiss you."

That grabbed Jameson's attention. Not the kiss. But the other part. "What kind of information?" he immediately asked.

"Same old stuff that everyone wants from me. Even though I was the one who hired Kelly, I think she accepted the job only so she could find out if I knew anything about your parents' murders. And the answer to that is what it's always been—I don't know anything about them, and I believe my brother is innocent. That means someone else killed them. The problem with that is you and your brother never did your jobs to find that other person."

Oh, they'd done their jobs all right. So had dozens of other cops and FBI agents. "All the evidence pointed to Travis."

"*Circumstantial* evidence," August spat out. "I believe Kelly was onto the real killer when she took that file from you."

This was an old argument, one that Jameson was tired of hearing. "That was *my* file she took, and there was nothing in there about someone else other than your brother killing my folks."

That wasn't entirely true. Jameson did have plenty of info on his father's active and past cases.

"Kelly used your file to make notes. Her own notes," August added.

She shook her head. "You read it?"

August suddenly got very quiet. "No, but you mentioned some of the things that were in it."

That sounded like a lie, and Jameson was about to press him on it when he heard the footsteps. So did August, and he turned in that direction.

"Mandy," August said on a rise of breath. "I didn't know you were in town."

Yeah, and Mandy was in a place Jameson didn't want her to be. He had intended for her to stay with Gracelyn and Erica, and Jameson stepped into the hall so he could watch the break room door. He definitely didn't want Erica bringing his daughter out here.

"You're hurt," August added, tipping his head to the bandage.

"I'm okay. You're here because of what's going on with Kelly and these hired guns?"

"In part. Boyer's on his way over with what I believe are warrants for my and Kelly's arrest." He paused again. "Do you know where his daughter is?"

"No." Mandy didn't hesitate. "And if Kelly knows, she doesn't remember."

"Yes," August said, glancing at Kelly. "Has your memory been returning? Can you recall anything about that file or Boyer's child?"

"Nothing about either of them," she assured him. "In fact, my memory might never return."

Jameson knew why she'd said that. If August was behind the attacks, she might believe that would get him to back off. It wouldn't. If there was anything in that file that could incriminate him, he would continue to go after it. Even if it meant killing Kelly. Or kidnapping Gracelyn to use her.

August's eyebrow lifted, and he stared at Kelly as if he expected her to say something different. Maybe the truth. That she was remembering and that it wouldn't be long before she figured out where she'd put that file.

And what was in it.

Finally, August gave up waiting and blew out a frustrated breath. "I heard there was another attack. Just a few hours ago."

"How did you hear that?" Kelly asked.

August lifted his shoulder. "I have friends at SAPD. I was at the prison visiting my brother when I heard, and I got here as fast as I could."

"You got here because Gabriel called you

in to answer questions about stalking Kelly," Jameson corrected.

The man's glare sharpened a bit more. "I would have come anyway. Whether they appreciate it or not, I care about what happens to Kelly and her sister. When they worked for me, they did everything they could to find evidence to free Travis. That's more than anyone else has done."

Clearly, that was meant as a dig at Jameson, but he didn't care. He took hold of Kelly's hand so he could lead her back to the break room. Mandy, too. That way, if they did have to leave, Jameson would be able to get her out of there, as well.

"Tomorrow is the anniversary of your parents' murders," August added when Jameson and Kelly started moving. Jameson motioned for Mandy to follow them. "If the real killer is out there, then he or she will almost certainly strike soon."

That stopped Jameson in his tracks. "You personally know something about that?"

"No. But I've been getting threatening letters and emails, too. Just like you and your family. Someone's out there and wants to finish what he or she started ten years ago, and for whatever reason, they've included me in this."

Jameson prayed that wasn't true, but August

was right about the threats. They were all getting them, and it was clear the violence was escalating. But August was right to question why he had been getting the threats. Unless it was to throw suspicion off himself.

Jameson got Kelly and Mandy walking toward the break room again, but this obviously wasn't his day for a quick exit. The front door opened, and Boyer stormed in. Or rather that's what he tried to do, but Gabriel was right there to block the agent's path by stepping in front of him. However, Jameson caught sight of something before his brother did that.

Boyer did indeed have some papers in his hand.

"Is it true?" Boyer asked. He wasn't looking at Gabriel, though. Instead, he was aiming his attention at Mandy.

Since Boyer looked ready to implode, Jameson moved in front of Kelly and her sister. "A lot of things are true," Jameson snarled, matching Boyer's tone. "Did you have something particular in mind?"

If looks could have killed, Jameson would be dead. "You know exactly what I'm talking about. You found a baby."

Jameson still had his hand on Kelly, and he felt her tense. He was certain he was doing some tensing, too. "Who told you that?" Jameson countered, and he hoped that Mandy or Kelly didn't blurt out anything. Best to fish for information rather than verify something he didn't want Boyer to know anyway.

"I heard," was all Boyer said. He didn't wait for Jameson to respond. "It's true." He groaned. "God, it's true. Where is she? I want to see her right now."

"We don't have your child." Jameson tipped his head to the papers Boyer was holding. "And if you're here to try to arrest Kelly and August, then you're wasting your time."

Boyer looked down at the papers, too, but his expression was odd. It was as if he'd forgotten they were there. He handed them to Gabriel.

"They're not arrest warrants," Boyer said. "Not yet anyway. The paperwork is for the transfer of a prisoner. McGill. I'm taking him into my custody."

"Why?" Jameson asked. He wanted to have a look at the papers, but he didn't want to leave Kelly in the hall with August. Plus, he didn't plan to get too far away from the break room.

"Justice Department business. I'm not at liberty to say."

"You mean you won't say." And Jameson could think of a bad reason for the agent's silence. "If McGill works for you—"

"He doesn't," Boyer interrupted. "But I'm taking him to headquarters to be interviewed."

By federal agents. Something was up, and Jameson hoped that didn't include Boyer trying to cover his tracks.

After reading through the papers, Gabriel looked back at Jameson. "Everything appears to be in order."

So either Boyer had bought off a judge or else there was a compelling reason for the feds to take McGill. Unfortunately, that meant the man wouldn't be around so Gabriel and the deputies could continue to press him for information. Information that could help them figure out who was orchestrating the attacks.

"Two marshals are on the way to transport the prisoner," Boyer added, and he looked at Mandy again. "Now tell me about the baby you found."

Gabriel got another call and stepped away to take it. Despite the fact that no one was now in his path, Boyer thankfully didn't come any closer. Maybe because all four of them—Jameson, Kelly, Mandy and August—were giving him looks from hell.

"She's not your daughter," Jameson settled for saying. No sense denying there was a child, since someone had obviously leaked details about not only the attack but the fact that Jameson and the others had left the crime scene with an infant.

"I don't believe you," Boyer snapped. "I want to see her *now*."

"No." Jameson had a quick debate with himself as to how to continue, and he just went with the truth. "She's my daughter. Mine and Kelly's."

"You had his child?" August asked.

Either August was genuinely surprised or else he was doing a good job of faking it. However, there was one emotion that August wasn't able to hide.

Jealousy.

Since Jameson had had a recent bout of it himself, he recognized it in August. The man's mouth stretched into a straight line.

Kelly nodded. "Jameson didn't know. I kept her from him because I was in hiding."

She hadn't added that it was also because she hadn't trusted him. But apparently she hadn't trusted August or Boyer, either.

Boyer took a couple steps toward them. Unlike August, there was no jealousy on his face, but there was emotion. And disbelief. The agent obviously thought they were lying.

"I want to see the baby," Boyer repeated. "If she's mine, I'll know it."

No way was he going to allow Boyer in the

break room or anywhere near Gracelyn for that matter. However, Jameson did take out his phone, and he quickly located the picture he'd taken of the baby a couple of hours earlier. He held it up so that Boyer could see.

Boyer eased the phone from Jameson's hand, his attention fixed to the smiling little girl on the screen. The moments crawled by before Boyer whispered "no" under his breath.

"You could have switched pictures of her." He thrust the phone back at Jameson. "That's why I have to see her for myself."

"You don't need to see her," Mandy verified. "Because I swear she's not yours."

Boyer groaned. The sound of a man in pain. Obviously, it was sinking in that they didn't have his child after all. "I can't give up hope," Boyer mumbled. "I have to find her."

The words had barely left his mouth when Gabriel walked back into the hall with them. "I just got a call from a criminal informant named Buddy Wells," Gabriel said. "He had something very interesting to tell me. Want to explain why we didn't hear it from you first?"

His brother hadn't directed that to Boyer or August. But rather to Mandy. Jameson expected her to be surprised by Gabriel's question.

She wasn't.

Mandy glanced away, dodging both Gabriel's

and his gaze, and she muttered some profanity that Jameson silently repeated.

"What is he talking about?" Kelly asked. When her sister didn't answer, she took hold of Mandy's chin, forcing eye contact. "What is it?" she demanded.

Mandy didn't answer, but Gabriel did. "Mandy is working for Boyer. Not only is she on his payroll, but Boyer and she are lovers."

Chapter Thirteen

Kelly waited for her sister to deny everything that Gabriel had just said. But Mandy didn't. Instead, she said something Kelly didn't want to hear.

"I'm sorry."

That felt like a punch to Kelly's gut. It didn't matter that her memories of Mandy were spotty at best; her sister hadn't been honest with her. And it instantly made Kelly wonder—what else had Mandy not told her?

Kelly looked at Boyer to see if he would have some kind of excuse. But even he wasn't denying it.

Oh, mercy.

What was really going on here?

Jameson stepped in front of Mandy, and he put his hands on his hips. "I'll want to hear more than an apology. I want a full explanation."

"So will I," August said.

All of them looked at the man, and they were likely wondering the same thing. Why would he care if Mandy and Boyer were lovers or not?

"I've been getting threats, and I believe at least some of them are coming from Boyer. Because I have PIs looking into what I believe are his dirty dealings. Mandy could have helped him cover up his crimes."

It was a stretch, especially since they didn't know any of the details of this bizarre relationship, but August could hope to try to use this—or anything else for that matter—to find something that would help clear his brother. After all, August believed that Boyer had something to do with setting up Travis.

"One of you had better start talking." Jameson shot warning glances at both Mandy and Boyer.

"It's true," Mandy finally said. She huffed. "After Kelly disappeared, Boyer hired me to find her."

For only a single sentence, it certainly packed a wallop. Kelly's breath became so thin that she got dizzy. She must have wobbled, because Jameson took hold of her arm to steady her.

"I didn't have anything to do with the attacks," Mandy quickly added.

Boyer stared at Mandy as if waiting for her to declare his innocence along with hers. But she didn't. "Nor did I," he said, his words clipped and tight. "And we were lovers. For a short time anyway."

So the affair was over. That didn't make Kelly feel any better, and judging from her sister's expression, she wasn't especially pleased about it, either.

Mandy huffed again. "Look, I know what you're thinking. Can you trust me? Well, you can. I'm not behind the attacks." She pointed to her bandaged arm. "I was shot, remember?"

"It was a flesh wound," Jameson said, taking the words right out of Kelly's mouth.

Her sister's gaze flew back to hers, and Mandy hissed out a breath when Kelly didn't jump to defend her. She couldn't. Maybe if she had her full memory back, she would know things that would convince her of Mandy's innocence. But for now, Kelly had to consider that her sister might have contributed to this dangerous situation they were in.

"Great." Mandy cursed. "You think I faked my kidnapping. I guess you believe I led those men to Gracelyn, too. I didn't."

Kelly knew this wasn't a debate they could decide here. Not with August seemingly lapping all of this up. He was probably trying to figure out a way to use it against Boyer. At the moment, though, Kelly didn't care about any of that. She had to get out of there.

"I need a drink of water," she lied, and she headed up the hall.

Jameson was right behind her, of course. They went into the break room, closed the door and immediately checked on Gracelyn. She was asleep in Erica's arms.

"We're leaving now," Jameson insisted before Kelly could say anything. He took out his phone and sent two texts. "I'd already started the arrangements for us to move, but I just had those plans stepped up a little. I'll have Cameron pull a cruiser to the back of the building. The four of us will go with him."

"Four?" Kelly repeated. "What about Mandy?"

His forehead bunched up, and he looked ready to launch into an argument as to why it wasn't a good idea to have Mandy go with them. But it wasn't an argument she needed.

"I don't want her to go with us, either," Kelly quickly added. "Not until we know what's going on." And that might not be for a while. "If my sister is completely innocent, then I'll owe her an apology."

Erica stood, cradling the baby in her arms. "Is something wrong with Mandy?"

Jameson and Kelly exchanged glances before he answered her question with one of his own.

"Did you know that Mandy was working for a federal agent?"

"No." She shook her head and repeated it. "I had no idea."

Too bad. Because Erica could have maybe filled in some memory gaps so that Kelly would know if she could trust her sister or not.

The door to the break room opened, and Kelly figured it was too much to hope that it was Gabriel or Cameron. It wasn't. It was Mandy, and she stepped in, shutting it behind her.

"I planned to tell you about Boyer," Mandy said right off. "But the timing wasn't right."

A soft burst of air left Kelly's mouth. "The timing was perfect for you to tell me that you work for one of our suspects."

"Worked," Mandy corrected. "I don't any longer." But she waved that off. "Fine. It's obvious I'm not going to be able to make you believe that my prior relationship with Boyer isn't playing into anything that's happening now."

"You're right. You won't be able to convince us, not now anyway," Jameson assured her. "I need to get Gracelyn and Kelly someplace safe, and then you can convince me you're innocent."

"I am innocent!" Mandy's voice was so loud that it woke up Gracelyn. The baby immediately started to fuss, so Kelly pulled Gracelyn into her arms. "Sorry," Mandy grumbled. "It's just that I'm in danger, too. I also need to be protected so the kidnappers can't have another go at me."

Mandy was right about that. If she had no part in the attacks, she could be taken again to try to force Kelly to cooperate. And cooperation probably meant handing over that blasted file.

Jameson nodded. "You will leave. Just not with Kelly, Erica and me. Susan will be here soon, and she and a reserve deputy will take you to a hotel. They'll stay with you until we can figure out what's going on."

Mandy opened her mouth, and Kelly didn't think it was her imagination that her sister was about to insist she go with them. But then Jameson's phone dinged with a text message, and he cut off anything she might have said.

"Cameron's in place. Let's go." Jameson looked at Mandy. "Just stay here and Susan will arrive soon." He didn't wait for Mandy to object. He hurried them out of there.

"Erica, get in the front," he instructed. Probably because there was a child seat in the middle of the back one.

Erica did get in, but it wasn't just Cameron in the front seat. There was another man, and he had Erica sit between them.

"That's Deputy Edwin Clary," Jameson said to Kelly. Maybe because he felt her tense. "We can trust him."

Good. But the fact that there were now three lawmen in the car let her know this could be a dangerous ride. She prayed they weren't attacked again.

The moment Kelly had the baby strapped in, Cameron took off, and Kelly saw the second cruiser pull to a stop behind the sheriff's office. That was no doubt Susan ready to whisk Mandy away. Maybe Mandy would cooperate.

Cameron sped up as soon as he was out of the parking lot. Blue River wasn't a big town by anyone's standards, so it only took them a couple minutes before they were away from the buildings. After he took a turn, there weren't any other vehicles in sight. It made it easier for Kelly to see if anyone was following them, but that didn't mean they were safe. This was a rural road, where gunmen could lie in wait.

A road she recognized.

"This leads to your family's ranch," she said.

Jameson's gaze had been firing all around them, but he glanced at her now. "Are you remembering that?"

She took another look at the scenery. Then nodded. "I didn't see much of it when you brought me here, but I remember it, too. From the other time I came here." It wasn't exactly a peaceful feeling, though, that went through her. "Won't our attackers expect you to take me there?"

"Maybe." That's all he said for several moments. "There are hands at the ranch who can help protect you. And it's only temporary. In the morning, we'll be going to a safe house."

The ranch would be more comfortable for Gracelyn than staying at the sheriff's office, but still she hated to bring the danger to Jameson's home.

"She'll be hungry soon," Erica said, turning in the seat so she could look at the baby. "I have some food for her in the diaper bag, but I'm not sure it's enough for more than a day or two."

"I'll arrange to have supplies brought in," Jameson assured her. "Just write down what you need. Not just for Gracelyn but for yourself, too."

Erica muttered a thanks, but she looked as worried about this as Kelly was. "At least once Gracelyn's eaten and had her bath," Erica went on, "she'll sleep through the night. Well, she usually does anyway. After Kelly left she had some fussy moments asking for her mama."

That ate away at Kelly, and it didn't matter that she couldn't remember leaving or much about her little girl. She just hated that she'd put Gracelyn and even Erica through that.

The drive seemed to take an eternity, but Kelly figured it was less than twenty minutes. She got more of those memory fragments the moment Cameron turned onto the ranch road.

"This is a different way we went from last night, but I've been this way before. Two years ago," she added.

Jameson nodded. He followed her gaze to the large house that was just up the road. Not someplace where anyone lived. Not anymore. But she knew that it was his parents' house. She had seen it earlier from a distance that morning after the first attack when Jameson had brought her to his house.

"There was a fire a while back," Jameson added.

Yes. And once they were closer, she could see the burned streaks on the wood on one side of the place. Even without the damage, it didn't look habitable. Maybe she felt that way, though, because two people had been murdered inside.

"We're finally tearing it down," he went on a moment later.

That was probably a wise move, but it made her wonder why the Becketts hadn't done it sooner. It was still their childhood home, so perhaps there were more good memories than bad.

Cameron pulled to a stop in front of another large house. But this one looked a little more like a fortress than a home. There were shutters that were all closed, and what appeared to be three armed ranch hands were standing guard.

"This is your house?" Erica asked.

Like Kelly, she was taking in the sprawling place surrounded by equally sprawling pastures. The Beckett Ranch was huge. Not a good thing right now. Because it might be hard to keep watch over every part of it to stop gunmen from getting onto the grounds.

"No. It's Gabriel's," Jameson answered. "My place is about a quarter of a mile past his."

"A log cabin," Kelly provided. Except *cabin* wasn't the right word. Like Gabriel's, it was huge, as well.

She suddenly had plenty of memories of it. Specifically of Jameson's bedroom. And his bed. It's where they'd had sex, and that might explain why he'd brought them here instead of there. It likely had memories for him, too.

"FYI, my sister Ivy is here," Jameson explained when Cameron pulled to a stop in front of the house. "My other sister, Lauren, is out of town on business, and she has two Texas Rangers with her as bodyguards. I told her it was best if she stayed away for a while."

It was. That would mean one less member of his family in danger.

Jameson smiled at Gracelyn when she opened her eyes and grinned at him. "And Gabriel's wife, Jodi, is here, too. Once we're inside, you might not get your hands on Gracelyn for a while. They'll want to get to know her."

"This isn't a good idea," Kelly said. She took the baby from the car seat.

Jameson didn't reassure her—probably because he wasn't so certain of this idea, either. But that didn't stop him from rushing them into the house. Cameron left the cruiser out front, and both Cameron and Edwin followed them in.

"We're staying," Cameron told her. "Gabriel's orders."

Gabriel was almost certainly stretched thin with his deputies, but Kelly was thankful there'd be three people guarding the baby. Apparently, there'd be a fourth, too, because the blond-haired woman who was in the foyer was wearing a shoulder holster.

"This is Jodi," Jameson said, making the introductions all the way around. "Jodi was in private security for years."

"Jodi Canton?" The name just came to Kelly, like one of those memory fragments. But this came with more than just a few pieces.

Jodi had been attacked the night Jameson's parents were murdered. Attacked and left for dead. She'd survived, but her father was none other than Travis Canton, who was in prison for a double murder.

"Yes," Jodi commented as if she knew exactly what Kelly had been thinking.

"You remember her?" Jameson asked.

Kelly shook her head. "No, I don't think we've ever met. But I saw pictures of her and read the articles." For some reason that was clearer in her mind than giving birth to her daughter.

Jodi didn't reach for the baby, but the woman who came from the adjacent living room did. The brunette made a beeline to Kelly and Gracelyn, and she gave them both a hug before she scooped up Gracelyn. This had to be Jameson's sister.

"She's a Beckett all right," Ivy said. "She resembles my son, Nathan. He's not here," she went on. "He's away at camp. His dad's there with him now just to make sure...well, just to make sure."

Again, that was smart. Because the person after her could use anyone to get to her.

"We don't have a crib here," Jodi explained. "It's at Cameron's house, where Lauren lives now. They have two kids so they needed it.

Anyway, we can have someone bring it up or maybe we could use a lot of quilts and make Gracelyn a bed on the floor."

Since Jodi knew the baby's name, that meant Jameson or Gabriel had filled her in on what was going on. Had probably told her about the memory loss, too, since both Jodi and Ivy eyed the bandage and gave her sympathetic looks.

"I'm sure the quilts will work fine," Kelly answered. "Plus, we're only here for one night."

"Where will you go after that?" Ivy asked her brother.

"A safe house. Not just for Gracelyn, Erica, Kelly and me. You and Jodi will be coming, too."

"Gabriel's orders," Cameron repeated while he kept watch at the front window.

Apparently, Kelly wasn't the only one who hadn't heard about this, because both Ivy and Jodi looked surprised.

"It's just a precaution," Jameson assured them. "And it'll give you some time to be with your niece."

"With Kelly, too." Ivy smiled and gave Kelly's hand a gentle squeeze. Her attention shifted to her brother, gauging his reaction to that, but Jameson glanced away. Perhaps that was his way of telling his sister that there was no reason to get to know Kelly because she wouldn't be around much.

The foyer suddenly got very quiet. Too quiet.

"Why don't I go ahead and feed the baby?" Erica suggested, obviously picking up on the uneasiness. She took Gracelyn from Ivy.

"I'll show you the kitchen," Jodi offered. "It's this way." She led Erica out of the foyer.

Kelly followed them, but Ivy caught up with her in the living room and caught on to her hand again. "Stay. You need to hear this, too."

Judging from Jameson's frown, he wasn't so sure of that. Neither was Kelly, but he joined them in the living room.

"I love you, and even though I just met her, I love my niece, too," Ivy started. She kept her voice at a whisper probably because Cameron still was in the foyer and Edwin was at the front window only yards away.

"But?" Jameson challenged.

"You can be pigheaded about some things, and my advice is don't let that get in the way of forgiving Kelly for not telling you about Gracelyn. I'm sure she had what she thought were solid reasons for not telling you."

Kelly wasn't sure how to respond to that. Ivy had really put her brother on the spot, and that's why she decided to stay quiet.

Jameson didn't, though.

"I have forgiven her," Jameson said. And he didn't say it in a whisper.

Kelly had been hit with a lot of emotional punches in the past two days, but that seemed one of the strongest. It didn't tighten her stomach, didn't cause her adrenaline to soar. However, it sent a new warmth through her.

Memories, too.

Of the feelings that had caused her to land in bed with Jameson. Of course, he probably still thought she'd done that to get her hands on the file. She hadn't. Nor had it been solely the attraction. It had been because she had deep feelings for him.

She still did.

"Well, maybe you're not as pigheaded as I thought you were," Ivy told him. "Oh, wait. You still are. You're just not being pigheaded about this." She poked him with her elbow and grinned in a way that only a sister could. "All right, let me have some playtime with my niece."

Ivy kissed Jameson's cheek. Then she did the same to Kelly before she headed off to the kitchen.

Jameson stared at her, maybe seeing how she was going to respond to what he'd said. And Kelly did. Despite the fact that Edwin and Cameron were nearby, she caught on to Jameson's arm, drew him closer and kissed him. Not on the cheek, either. She went for broke. Because if this was a mistake, she wanted it to be one worth making.

The taste of him roared through her. Now, here was another of those punches, but it was a good one, too. That taste mixed with the now-familiar heat. All of it slid right through her. And though things were far from perfect, it all suddenly felt right.

She pulled back to gauge his reaction. The corner of his mouth lifted in what looked to be a smile. Good. Well, almost. That ghost of a smile vanished as quickly as it'd come. He was already regretting the kiss. Maybe regretting, too, that he had forgiven her.

He opened his mouth to say something, and then it seemed as if he changed his mind. Jameson slid a glance at Edwin. The deputy had his attention focused on looking out the window, but he was also making occasional glances over his shoulder at them. In other words, this wasn't the time for a heartfelt private conversation. Or a kiss, for that matter.

"Let's check on Gracelyn," Jameson finally said.

That made Kelly smile. The thought of her baby could do that to her. Jameson and she started for the kitchen just as his phone buzzed, and she saw Gabriel's name on the screen. Jameson stopped and took the call, putting it on speaker.

"We got a problem," Gabriel greeted.

Kelly groaned, because they'd already had way too many problems today. She prayed it wasn't news of gunmen on the way to the ranch.

"Mandy was furious after you left," Gabriel continued a moment later. "At first she refused to go with the deputies, but I finally told her if she didn't, I'd have to lock her up. She's a witness after all."

Mandy was indeed that, but Kelly figured her sister probably hadn't cared much for the lockup threat. "What did Mandy do?" Kelly came out and asked.

"She escaped."

Kelly's next groan wasn't of frustration but concern. It wasn't safe for her sister to be out there. Judging from Jameson's profanity, he felt the same way.

"We have someone looking for her," Gabriel went on, "but I don't have a lot of manpower to search for long."

"You need Cameron or Edwin to go back to the station?" Jameson asked.

"No," Gabriel answered without hesitation. "They need to stay put and keep watch. All of you do." He paused. "Before Mandy escaped, she said she needed to find Kelly and settle some things with her."

That sent a chill through Kelly. Because it sounded like a threat.

"Oh, and be careful," Gabriel added a moment later. "There's a gun missing from my desk, and I'm pretty sure Mandy took it. She's armed, and I'm betting the first place she'll go is the ranch."

Chapter Fourteen

Jameson glanced at the clock on the nightstand before turning his attention back to the window. It was just past midnight. That meant it was officially the anniversary of his parents' murders.

Since he could see the old house where they'd died from the window, that wasn't exactly a calming thought, or sight, to settle his nerves, which were already on edge.

Neither was the fact that Jameson was second-and third-guessing himself about coming here. It wasn't just the danger—that would be a factor no matter where they'd gone. But having Kelly here was reminding him of old feelings for her that he'd thought were long gone.

They weren't.

And now she was under the same roof he was. In fact, she was just next door. Mere steps away. Steps that he forced himself not to take. For one thing, he wanted to keep watch a while longer. There'd been no sign of Mandy, or anyone else for that matter, but Jameson figured it would help to have an extra pair of eyes on the grounds just in case someone did try to come after them.

However, there were other reasons for him to stay put. Any time Kelly and he were within ten feet of each other, the heat kicked in, and Jameson found himself making questionable choices.

Like kissing her.

And wanting much more than just a kiss from her.

He felt his body tighten and respond to that thought, and a certain part of him was urging him to go see her. Jameson told that part to take a hike. After all, Kelly wasn't alone in the room, and she might even be sleeping. Even if she wasn't, he could still wake up Erica or the baby.

Gabriel's house was huge, six bedrooms, but with all the "guests," it'd practically taken a flowchart to work out the sleeping situations. Jodi was in the master, where Gabriel would join her whenever he happened to make it home from work. Ivy and Jameson were in two of the guest rooms. Cameron was in another guest room, where he was resting to take the surveillance shift over from Edwin. Erica and Kelly had decided to share a room with the baby since

Kelly wasn't exactly confident of her mothering skills just yet.

His phone buzzed, and Jameson answered it right away when he saw Gabriel's name on the screen. "Mandy hasn't shown," Jameson volunteered.

"Good. Maybe she'll stay away. Are you okay?"

There'd been enough of a hesitation before his brother's question to let Jameson know what that was really about. Their parents. Gabriel had no doubt been watching the clock, too.

"That old house needs to come down," Jameson settled for saying.

"Agreed." Another hesitation. "Do you ever think August could be right, that Travis could be innocent?" Obviously, the anniversary of the murders had put his brother in a contemplative mood.

"All the time," Jameson admitted. "I wish Travis could just remember what happened that night. Gaps in memories, especially those kind of memories, aren't a good thing."

"Are you talking about Kelly now?" Gabriel asked.

"Yeah." Now it was Jameson who hesitated. "I have feelings for her."

It sounded as if Gabriel laughed. "And you're just now figuring that out. You're slower than I thought you were. Still, I get what you're saying. Feelings don't always make things easier."

No, and Gabriel was a living example of that. After all, he'd fallen in love with Travis Canton's daughter. And Ivy had fallen in love with Travis's son and had a child with him. In the grand scheme of things, Jameson's relationship with Kelly was far less complicated than theirs. Or at least it would be if she had her full memory.

"I had another reason for calling," Gabriel said a moment later. "I'm sending you a picture. I think this might be Boyer's daughter, Amy."

Of all the things Jameson had thought his brother might say, that wasn't one of them. With everything else going on, Boyer's child wasn't even on Jameson's radar. He waited a few seconds for the photo to come through, and he saw the blond-haired little girl. She was obviously a little older than Gracelyn and looked healthy.

"I pressed the CI who told me about Mandy and Boyer," Gabriel continued, "and he's the one who came up with the picture."

Jameson had a lot of questions, but he started with the obvious. "Where has the baby been this whole time? And who took her?" Before Gabriel could answer, there was a knock at the door. "Hold on a second."

He hurried to answer the knock just in case it was one of the deputies with bad news. But it was Kelly. She was standing there, not looking at all certain that she should be there. She glanced around, rubbing her hands along the sides of her jeans. Clearly nervous.

Jameson figured he seemed uncertain, too. But only because he was surprised. His body certainly liked the idea of her paying him a late-night visit.

"Gabriel's on the phone," he explained to her. Jameson motioned for her to come in so he could shut the door. That way, their conversation wouldn't disturb the others. "He just sent me a picture of a child who could be Boyer's. He got it from the CI." He showed it to her, and Kelly's eyes widened.

"As for where the child has been for two years," Gabriel went on, "the CI didn't know that. He got the picture from the baby's nanny. A woman he knows only as Sissy. But as to who had her, well, the CI claims it was Mandy."

Hell. This was not a twist that Jameson wanted to hear. Neither did Kelly, and she groaned and shook her head.

"The CI is certain?" Kelly asked. She joined Jameson at the window.

"He says he is, but he's a criminal informant.

Emphasis on the *criminal*. But he was right about Mandy and Boyer being lovers."

Yeah, he was. But that only led Jameson to another question. "Why would Mandy take Boyer's child?"

"Don't know, but it's something I intend to ask her when we find her. I'll ask Boyer, too, but I'm going to wait until morning to do that. Get some sleep," Gabriel added.

"You should do the same," Jameson said right back to him. "When will you be home?"

"In a couple of hours. Be safe," Gabriel tacked on before he ended the call.

Jameson took another look at the picture before he put his phone away. "I'm sorry," he said in case she was upset about what she'd just heard.

Kelly lifted her shoulder. "I don't remember a lot about my sister, so I don't know if she's capable of taking the baby. Especially considering she had a relationship with Boyer."

It sounded as if she had plenty of distrust for Mandy. Even if it turned out to be unwarranted, in their case it was better to be safe than sorry. That's why he didn't want Mandy to get near Kelly or the baby.

"I wanted to check on you. To make sure you were okay." Her gaze drifted to the old house before Jameson moved her back away from the glass. The odds were the ranch hands or deputies would spot a gunman before he could strike, but like having Mandy around, it was an unnecessary risk.

"Gabriel wanted to know the same thing. Yeah, I'm fine," he repeated to her.

She stared at him. "You're lying."

He hated that she could see through him so easily. Most would have bought that lie. "Once the anniversary has passed, maybe the threats will stop."

Of course, the threats could get a whole lot worse before they ended, but Jameson didn't spell that out for her. She knew.

"Is Gracelyn okay?" he asked.

She nodded. "Erica says she'll likely sleep through the night. I was on the pallet on the floor with her, but she never even opened an eye or stirred around."

Good. Though she was probably the only one in the house who would get much sleep.

It suddenly got too quiet, and Jameson could think of plenty of things they could talk about. The investigation. The safe house where they'd soon be going. Or how they were going to work out custody arrangements for Gracelyn. But before he could say anything, Kelly fluttered her fingers to the door.

"I should leave," she said, her voice showing

some strain. She dragged in a long breath. "But if I do, I'll just want to come back over here."

He knew exactly what she meant. "It's because I kissed you. It brought back a lot of old stuff to the surface." And it brought it back with a vengeance.

Cursing himself, Jameson slipped his arm around her neck, pulled her to him and kissed her again.

Even though he'd been the one to start this, it still gave him a jolt. The feel of her in his arms. The need she created inside him. He kissed her too hard. Too long. And yet it didn't feel like nearly long enough when they broke apart for air. Jameson would have gone right back for another kiss, too, if his phone hadn't buzzed again.

He glanced at the screen, expecting it to be Gabriel again, but the caller had blocked the number.

Hell.

"The gunmen," Kelly said, her breathing already too fast.

It probably was one of them, and that's why Jameson moved her even farther away from the window. "If things get bad, take Gracelyn into the bathroom and get in the tub with her."

Kelly gave a shaky nod, and he hit the answer button. However, it was a familiar voice.

It was Mandy.

"I need to talk to Kelly," the woman immediately said.

"I'm here," Kelly answered before Jameson could consider if that was a good idea or not. Of course, Mandy would have known Kelly would be with him.

"Where are you?" Jameson demanded.

"As if I'd tell you that. You two obviously don't trust me, and that's why I'm calling. I'm not responsible for what's going on. I didn't do anything wrong."

Jameson wasn't so sure of that at all. "What about taking Boyer's daughter?"

Silence. For too long of a time. "That was a mistake."

"A mistake?" Kelly repeated. "You took a man's child. A man who's a federal agent. And don't say you didn't know he was one because Boyer insisted that he told us."

"He did," Mandy reluctantly admitted. He heard her give a heavy sigh. "But Hadley convinced me that he was bad news, that he wasn't fit to raise the child. She said he was a dangerous man."

"Hadley might have been right," Jameson said. "But you committed a felony."

This time Mandy groaned. "I know, and

that's why I haven't given her back. Because I'll go to jail."

Jameson wanted to point out that she deserved to be locked up, but if Boyer truly was dangerous, then maybe Mandy had done the right thing.

Maybe.

And if so, he would help her work her way through the legalities of this. But only after he was certain she wasn't the one who was after Kelly.

"Tell me what happened between Boyer and you," Kelly insisted.

"Nothing much to tell. It was just sex."

Jameson had to mentally shake his head. "But you just said you didn't know if he was a dirty agent."

"Not at the beginning. Not after his daughter was born. Later, though, things just sort of happened between us, and before you say it shouldn't have—I already know that. That's why I broke it off." Mandy paused. "I think Boyer was using me anyway. He was always pressing me for info about Kelly and that damn file she stole."

Yeah, that. Jameson certainly hadn't forgotten about it. "Were you telling the truth when you said you didn't know where it was?"

"Yes," Mandy answered without hesitation.

"Kelly vanished without so much as a word. She didn't trust me to help her."

Jameson heard the hurt—and the bitterness—and he had to wonder if there was enough hurt to give Mandy a motive for coming after Kelly. Or maybe all of this was just a ploy to get her hands on the file so she could give it to Boyer.

"Mandy, you need to tell us where you are," Kelly said. "That way, we can get you some protection."

"No." She sounded adamant about it, too. "I've got to look into some things."

Kelly shook her head, clearly not liking the sound of that. "What things?"

"Just some things I have to do. I'm sorry, Kelly, but what I'm about to do might make it more dangerous for you. For others, too. I might be handing you over to a killer."

And with that warning hanging in the air, Mandy ended the call.

KELLY COULD ONLY stand there and stare at the phone. Oh, God. What had her sister done? Worse, what was she going to do to stop whatever it was Mandy was planning?

"I won't let Mandy hand you over to anyone," Jameson assured her. He sounded exactly like the tough lawman that he was. But maybe no one was tough enough to save her.

She felt the tears burn her eyes and blinked them back. Or rather she tried. "You could die trying to protect me. I don't want that to happen."

"I don't have any plans to die." He blew out a weary breath, and maybe because he'd spotted those stupid tears, Jameson slipped his arm around her waist and pulled her back to him.

Not for a kiss this time. He just stood there and hugged her. All in all, it was an effective way to comfort her. Some anyway. There'd be no real comfort until the person responsible for the attacks was in jail.

Even if that meant putting her sister in prison.

"I'll bet you're regretting I came back into your life," she muttered.

He didn't answer right away, but he did ease back so that he was looking her in the eyes. "I'm not regretting it nearly enough."

It was a puzzling answer, but Kelly didn't even have time to process it before his mouth came to hers. Unlike the kiss that'd happened minutes earlier, this one was gentle. Like a whisper. So soft that there was no urgency in it. No demands. Just one incredible kiss. Of course, all of Jameson's kisses fell into the incredible category.

"If you leave now, we won't do something we might regret," he said with his mouth still against hers.

It sounded as if he was having the same debate with himself that she was. True, if she left, they wouldn't have sex. That might help them stay focused on the investigation. But leaving didn't exactly feel like an option.

And that's why Kelly pulled him back to her for another kiss.

She knew the kiss wasn't going to make this decision easier. Just the opposite. But she was tired of having this panic rising inside her. Tired of wanting Jameson more than her next breath. Sex wouldn't fix that. However, it could give them a reprieve from the relentless pressure. This heat, too.

He made a sound. Almost a protesting grumble. That didn't stop him, though, from snapping her even closer to him. Until her body was right against his. Kelly could already feel him hard and ready behind his zipper, and while she hadn't needed anything else to fire up every inch of her, that did it.

She had been the one to start the kiss, but Jameson seemed to be on a mission to finish it. He turned her, pinning her against the wall so he could lower those kisses to her neck. Then, lower. He kissed her breasts, first through her top, and then he shucked it off. Her bra, too.

The pleasure spiked through her when his mouth landed on her bare skin. The memories spiked as well, and she recalled another time they'd done this. It all came flooding back, the new images filling in the gaps, and she remembered in perfect detail the last time they'd been together. That didn't cool the fire. Just the opposite. Because she remembered what Jameson was capable of doing to her.

With the need building and building inside her, Kelly reached between them to unbutton his shirt. Jameson helped by taking off his shoulder holster, but it still took some more fumbling on her part to get the shirt off him.

He immediately came back for another kiss, and she got the pleasure of feeling his bare chest against hers. Yes, that was another pleasant memory, too, and they were making more of those memories right now.

The kiss made things better. And worse. Better because it was so good but worse because it made her realize she had to have him now. Thankfully, Jameson was on the same page, and the battle started to get them undressed. They managed the jeans before Kelly froze.

"Please tell me you have a condom," she said.

Jameson cursed, and for a moment she

thought that meant he didn't. But he stooped down, fumbling with his jeans, and finally came up with one from his wallet. The relief came, briefly, but the pressure-cooker heat quickly took over again.

Kissing her, Jameson pulled her to the floor, moving on top of her. It seemed to take forever for him to get on the condom, but even a few seconds seemed like way too long. Not with this need she had eating away at her.

She got another slam of memories when he pushed inside her. Yes, she definitely remembered this, and it didn't take her long to slide right into the rhythm of his movements. Of course, this would all end too soon. No way could it last with them starved for each other.

Jameson upped the pace, moving inside her until Kelly could take no more. Even though she wanted to hang on to this as long as possible, she had no choice. She had to let go. She felt herself shatter. Felt the pleasure ripple through her. It rippled through Jameson as well, because he gathered her into his arms and surrendered right along with her.

It was perfect. The slack feeling in her body. Jameson's taste in her mouth. His scent on her body. But in that moment, Kelly had a stark realization. This wasn't going to satisfy that fire inside her.

Not for long anyway.

The need would return, but that didn't mean she wouldn't have Jameson again. No. It wouldn't take long for the regret to take hold of him. Kelly was certain that's what was already happening when he moved off her and landed on his back on the floor.

"We should check on Gracelyn," he said. He turned toward her, hauled her back to him and kissed her. "Give me a minute, and we can do that."

So maybe not regret after all. He gathered up his clothes and headed to the en suite bathroom. Since Kelly really didn't want to be lying around on the floor naked, she dressed, too. She braced herself for some awkwardness when Jameson came back into the room, but there wasn't any.

Probably because he kissed her again. His kisses had a way of tamping down everything but the attraction. Not only was it still there, but it was stronger than ever.

"I remembered some things," she said while she put on her shoes.

That got his attention. "What?" he asked, hesitation in his voice.

"Us being together." Which probably wasn't much of a surprise since she'd had plenty of visual reminders what with seeing Jameson naked.

But that wasn't all.

It didn't come to her in a flash as the last pieces had, but it came, and she had to shake her head. "I didn't steal that file for Boyer. In fact, I wasn't the one who took it at all. Mandy did. She's the one who brought it to me."

"What?" He pulled his eyebrows together. "But she said you stole it." He paused. "No, wait. Mandy didn't say that. When she was talking to you, she said *as soon as you got your hands on it*. I guess that means she gave it to you?"

Yes, her sister had used some clever wording, but with each passing second the memories of that were getting clearer.

"I took it from her," Kelly corrected. "Mandy had sneaked into your house the night we were together and she took the file back to her apartment. The following morning, I dropped by her apartment and saw her reading it. I was furious and took it from her." Now it was her turn to pause. "I wonder if she shared any of what was inside it with Boyer?"

Judging from the frustrated sound he made, the answer to that was yes. But that led Kelly to one very big question.

Why was that file so important?

"I went through all the data you'd collected," Kelly went on, "and I added some files and notes of my own. I'd also talked with some possible witnesses and such. I had even interviewed one of the people involved in the money laundering operation that both Boyer and your father were investigating. I'd intended to take everything to you, but then someone attacked me when I went out to my car and I ran."

Jameson took a moment, clearly processing all of that. "Someone must have thought you learned something pretty damn important to try to kill you. Did you?"

She had to shake her head. "But I had the feeling that something was there. Some kind of…inconsistency."

"I know what you mean. I had the same feeling. That's why I kept digging." He paused again. "Tell me about that chat you had with the money launderer."

Kelly blew out a frustrated breath. "The guy's name was Lionel Rouse."

"Yeah, I tried to talk to him, too, but he wouldn't see me. My father had been investigating him."

"Yes, that was in your notes. I'm not sure why Lionel agreed to see me. Maybe because he thought I would help him get out of jail. Anyway, he said the wrong man was behind bars. I asked him who should be, and he said it was the head honcho. He wouldn't say more so I started looking for a money trail, something that would tell me who'd paid off this guy. Nothing."

"But the man or woman who paid him could have believed you found something."

His phone rang, cutting off anything else he might have added to that, and Jameson frowned, then cursed, when he saw the unfamiliar number on the screen. He answered it but didn't say anything. However, it didn't take long for the caller to speak.

"I'm so sorry." It was Mandy, and her words were rushed together. "I really screwed up, and you have to help me."

"What's wrong?" Jameson snapped.

"Some men took Amy. They have Boyer's daughter, and they took her to your family's ranch. God, Jameson, you have to save her."

Chapter Fifteen

Kelly stared at Jameson's phone, praying that she had misheard what her sister said. But Mandy's earlier words came back to her.

What I'm about to do might make things more dangerous for you. For others, too.

Had Mandy been talking about Boyer's child then? If so, if those kidnappers had actually gotten their hands on her and brought her to the ranch, then yes, a lot of people were suddenly in danger.

Not just Amy, either, but Gracelyn and everyone else in Gabriel's house.

Her sister was sobbing. Kelly had no trouble hearing that. But she also knew that sobs could be faked. She hated to distrust Mandy, but there were too many unanswered questions about her sister's relationship with one of their top suspects. Now that suspect's child had supposedly been taken.

"Mandy, what happened?" Jameson demanded.

He hurried to the window to look out. "How'd kidnappers get to the baby?"

There was another sob. "I had her in a safe place, and I managed to borrow a car and drive out there. But there was a tracking device on my shoe. The men who kidnapped me must have put it there when they knocked me out, and I must have missed it when we checked yesterday. They followed me there and took her. Please, just get her from them. They'll hurt her to get to Kelly."

Kelly couldn't help but react to that. Those monsters could have a precious baby. It didn't matter that it was someone else's child; the emotion hit Kelly as hard as if the little girl were her own.

"What do you think I can do to get her back?" Jameson asked, the frustration and concern in his voice.

"I don't know." Mandy was sobbing so hard now that it was difficult to understand her. "But you have to do something. You have to get to her before they hurt her."

Jameson kept his attention on the grounds outside the window. "I don't see anyone other than a couple of my ranch hands. Stay on the line while I text one of the deputies. I can have everyone keep an eye out for anything suspicious. You're sure the men will bring the baby here?"

"That's what they said. They hit me with a stun gun, tied me up and took her, but I could still hear what they were saying. As soon as I was able to move and get out of the ropes, I started driving to the ranch. But they're a good hour ahead of me. In fact, they could be there by now."

Kelly tried to see all possible angles of this, but it was hard to think. Not with this new round of panic coursing through her. "Was there a nanny or someone with Amy?"

"A nanny. They used a stun gun on her, too. I didn't bring her with me," Mandy added. "This is going to be dangerous, and there was no need to put her in the middle of it."

Kelly didn't like the sound of that. "The middle of it? What are you going to do?"

"Get back the baby," Mandy insisted. "I'll be there as fast as I can."

Jameson cursed again when Mandy hung up, but he didn't try to call her back. Instead, he called Cameron and filled him in on what was happening.

"Go ahead and tell Gabriel so he can get out here. You and Edwin should stay put for now, but I might need you to get Gracelyn and the others out of here in the cruiser."

She couldn't hear what Cameron said in response to that because Kelly's heartbeat was drumming in her ears. She did want her baby far from here, but that came with huge risks. Just getting in the cruiser meant they'd have to be outside. Even a few seconds in the open could give a gunman a chance to shoot them.

"I can't be with Gracelyn in the cruiser," Kelly said the moment Jameson finished his call with Cameron. "I can't do anything that will make her a target." And that's exactly what anyone with her would be.

The muscles stirred in Jameson's jaw. He was probably trying to think of an argument to counter that. There wasn't one. It was true the men might try to get to Gracelyn to get Kelly to cooperate, but she believed the men wouldn't go after the baby if Kelly was still on the ranch where they could get to her.

"It might not even come to that," Jameson assured her. He brushed a kiss on her cheek. "Go tell Erica, Jodi and Ivy what's going on. Jodi can get guns for all of you. I'm sure there's a stash in the house. Then the four of you should take Gracelyn into the bathroom and wait for me there. I won't be long. I just need to talk with some of the ranch hands."

Part of her hated being tucked away while Jameson and the deputies were in possible harm's way, but the bathroom would be the safest place for Gracelyn.

She turned to hurry out, but Kelly gave Jameson one last look. There was already a sinking feeling in the pit of her stomach, and she hoped this wasn't the last time they would see each other. Pushing that thought aside, she went to the bedrooms and alerted the others.

Jodi was already up and on the phone. "Gabriel's on the way," she relayed, tucking a gun into the back waist of her jeans. "Any sign of the kidnappers?"

Kelly had to shake her head, and she took another gun that Jodi grabbed for her from the nightstand. Jodi got Ivy while Kelly went to the bedroom to get Erica and the baby moving. Like Jodi, Erica was awake as well and had already scooped up Gracelyn in her arms. The nanny reached to turn on the light, but Kelly stopped her.

"It's just a precaution," Kelly told Erica when she saw that the woman was shaking, and Kelly prayed that was true.

Erica got in the bathtub with Gracelyn, but Kelly went to the only window in the room. Like the ones in Jameson's room, this one faced the old house. It was dark, though, with only a watery moon, and it was hard to see much of anything. Though she did spot a rifle-toting ranch hand just below them.

There were footsteps in the hall, and Jodi

automatically pivoted in that direction. But it was only Ivy and Jameson. Ivy went to the tub after Jameson motioned for her to do that, and he went to the window with Jodi and her.

"The hands are in place," Jameson explained. "There are six guarding the house and the rest are walking the perimeter, and they've had eyes on the cruiser the entire time we've been here. No one could have tampered with it."

Good. Because if they had to use it to escape, Kelly didn't want there to be a tracking device on it.

Jameson moved both Jodi and her to the side of the window just as his phone buzzed. It wasn't Mandy, though. This time there was a name on the screen.

Boyer.

"Is it true?" Boyer asked the moment Jameson answered. Unlike his call to Cameron, he put this one on speaker and continued to keep watch. "Do the men who are after Kelly really have my daughter?"

Boyer certainly sounded like a frantic father in fear for his child. But like Mandy's sobs, those emotions could be faked.

"I can't say for sure," Jameson answered, "but we're looking out for them. How did you find out?"

"The kidnappers called me."

Kelly had been certain Mandy had gotten in touch with him. And again, she might have. She reminded herself that this could all be a ruse. At the moment, Kelly couldn't trust either of them.

"What did the kidnappers say?" Jameson asked.

"That they were at your ranch, in the house where your parents were murdered. Are they?"

Because she was close enough to Jameson, she could feel the muscles in his arm tense. "I don't see them. That doesn't mean they aren't there."

Sweet heaven. He was right. There were thick woods behind the house, and the kidnappers could have gotten in that way.

"I'm on my way there now," Boyer added. "If you see my daughter, get her away from those SOBs."

Jameson didn't argue with the man. Probably because he knew there was nothing he could say to stop him. If Boyer was truly a father terrified for his child's life, then he would come no matter what. If he was the person behind the attacks, then he could already be on the grounds. Added to that, Jameson's phone dinged, indicating he had another call coming in.

"I've got to go," Jameson told Boyer, and Kelly saw Unknown Caller on the screen. Probably Mandy. Jameson must have thought so, too, because he quickly answered it.

But it wasn't Mandy.

"I'm gonna make this real short and sweet," the man said. "I got a kid here at your folks' place. A cute little girl."

No. It was the kidnapper. Kelly automatically looked at the old house again, but she still didn't see anyone.

"How do we know for sure that you actually have her?" Jameson asked. "I'll want some kind of proof, something more than just the sounds of her crying."

There was a pause, some chatter, and several moments later, Jameson's phone dinged. "Just sent you a picture. Told you she was cute."

Kelly looked at the screen when the picture loaded. It did indeed seem to be the same little girl in the photo Gabriel had sent them. "Is that your parents' house in the background?" she whispered to Jameson.

He nodded. "That's the family room," he mouthed.

She hadn't exactly doubted the men when they'd told them their location, but it seemed to be true. The kidnappers were just up the path from them.

"What do you want?" Jameson snarled to them.

"Well, I want your lady friend, Kelly. You

see, that's the only way you're gonna get back this cute little girl."

Even with the dim light, Kelly saw Jameson's eyes narrow and his jaw go stiff. "You're not getting Kelly."

"I figured you'd say that, and that's why I want her to make the decision. Put her on the phone."

Jameson shook his head, obviously not wanting her to say anything, but the kidnappers would have known she would be with him. "I'm here," she said.

"Good. Now we can have a real heart-to-heart." The kidnapper's tone had a sickening sweetness to it. "Are you the kind of woman who can live with herself if you caused an innocent little girl to be hurt or worse? I doubt you are. And that's why you'll do the right thing."

"And what is the *right* thing?" No sweetness to Jameson's voice. It had that lethal lawman's edge now.

"Start walking to the house, and it's okay if Kelly brings you with her. But only you. One cowboy is more than enough for this little adventure. Talk it out with each other and make your decision. But make it quick. I'll call back in five minutes, and I'll expect an answer. Oh, and I'm expecting that answer to be yes, or you'll hear a lot more of this."

The sound shot through Kelly as if a bullet had slammed into her.

Because the sound she heard was a baby's cry.

JAMESON HAD HOPED that all of this was a hoax. But he was pretty sure those cries were real. Of course, the kidnappers could be using a recording of Boyer's baby—or any baby for that matter—but he had to assume they did indeed have the child.

And the child was now in grave danger.

"Five minutes," the kidnapper repeated, and he ended the call.

He looked at Kelly, and Jameson knew what she was going to say even before she said it. "I have to go out there," she insisted.

She probably knew what he was going to say, too. "They'll kill you."

There were no doubts in his mind that's exactly what would happen. Well, it would after they tortured her to tell them the location of that file. After they had that, they would have no more need for her.

The thought of that twisted away at him. Hell. He had to figure out a way to stop this from happening. He considered calling Gabriel, but that would only waste those precious seconds that were already ticking away. He could fill in his brother after he set some things in motion. Instead, Jameson called Cameron.

"Have four of the hands go to the old house," Jameson explained. "The kidnappers say they're holding Boyer's baby there. A baby they want to exchange for Kelly."

Cameron cursed. "I'll have the hands start moving now."

"I want them to keep out of sight if possible." Jameson doubted it was. Those goons probably had the whole ranch under surveillance. "And tell them to be careful. I don't want any of them shot."

Cameron assured him he would, and Jameson hung up so that the deputy could get started on that.

"Will the hands make it there before our time is up?" Kelly asked.

"No." He hated the look that came on her face. Because it was a look of surrender. "But I want them in place to back us up if all else fails."

He hoped like the devil that it didn't come to that, though.

"You're not going out there," Ivy said. Jameson hadn't even known she'd heard the conversation, but she obviously had.

"We won't go out there on the kidnappers' terms," Jameson assured her. "When they call back, I'll negotiate it so that I go instead of Kelly. I'll tell them that she told me the location of the file." He glanced at her. "Do you know where it is?"

She must have remembered something because she nodded. "A safe-deposit box in San Antonio. We could just tell them that, and it might put an end to things."

It wouldn't. "Whoever hired those men won't want you alive. Because you know what's in the files."

"It's the same for you," Kelly quickly pointed out.

"No. I've only seen the portion of the file I created. I don't know the other things you added to it."

That part was true. But that didn't mean the kidnappers would believe him and keep him alive. Still, he was a lawman, trained in self-defense, and he might be able to overpower them and escape with the baby.

Jameson didn't want to think of all the things that could go wrong with a plan like that.

Even though Kelly had known the kidnappers would call back, the sound of his phone buzzing shot through the room, causing her to gasp. It certainly didn't ease the knot in his gut, but he answered it, praying he would be able to pull this off.

"Well?" the kidnapper said. The guy still had that smug tone that made Jameson want to punch him until he could no longer taunt them.

"I'll come to the house. Once we have the baby and we verify that she's okay, I'll give you the location of the file."

Silence, and the moments crawled by. Jameson could hear the kidnapper have a muffled conversation with someone, but he couldn't tell if that person was also in the house or if he or she was on another phone line.

"No can do," the kidnapper finally said. "We need Kelly to come to us. Oh, and if I were you, I wouldn't risk any deputies or those men who work for you. That's because we've set up explosives around the perimeter of the house. One wrong step, and they go kaboom."

That kicked up Jameson's pulse a significant notch. Kelly's, too. He heard the sharp intake of her breath and saw her hands begin to tremble.

"You're lying," Jameson told the man. "When would you have had time to set up explosives?"

"Oh, we've had them there for nearly two days now. We sneaked in when you were all tied up at the hospital with Kelly, tending her boo-boos. We had everything in place, and a *friend* just brought in the baby from one of the back trails."

With all the insanity that'd been going on for the past two days, it wouldn't have been that hard for someone to come onto the ranch and get into the house. Still, he wanted to kick himself for letting that happen. He should have put guards on the house. Hell, on the entire ranch.

"So here's what we want," the kidnapper went on. "Kelly comes out of the front of the house and starts walking on the trail toward us. No guns. Of course, she'll probably have one hidden away somewhere, but if we see the gun, we start shooting. Not at her, either."

Jameson wanted to reach through the phone and tear this idiot to bits. Because that was a not-so-veiled threat to hurt the baby.

"Who knows, some of those shots could get into your brother's house, where you've got your own kid and family stashed away," the kidnapper added. "Wouldn't want that, would we?"

No. They wouldn't. It would take a long-range rifle for someone to fire into Gabriel's place, but it could be done.

The kidnapper continued a moment later. "Like I said earlier, you can come with her, cowboy. But if you're not at the old house in ten minutes, well, you know what will happen."

"The baby is their leverage," Jameson told Kelly the moment the thug ended the call. "They won't do anything to her."

Jameson hoped that was true anyway, but the main reason he'd said it was to get the stark look off Kelly's face. It didn't work. She was still terrified, still shaking, but that didn't stop her from moving. She hurried to the tub and kissed Gracelyn. Their daughter was still asleep, thank God. No way did Jameson want her to hear any of this.

Including her mother's goodbye.

Kelly didn't exactly say the words, but it was obvious that's what she was doing. Because she might not get out of this alive. Jameson kissed the baby, as well. However, he didn't intend for this to be a farewell. Somehow he was going to make sure Kelly survived.

"You don't have to do this," Jameson told Kelly when she started out of the room. "I can go alone and negotiate with them once we're face-to-face." Of course, that was a serious long shot, and judging from the skeptical sound Kelly made, she knew that, as well.

"It's too big of a risk." She tucked her gun in the back waist of her jeans and headed down the stairs.

It was a huge risk, but Jameson had to try. He

also needed to take a few more precautions and hope they would be enough. Nothing would be as safe as he wanted it to be, but at this point he didn't have time to figure out a better way to get close enough to those men to get back the baby.

He stopped by Gabriel's home office and found the Kevlar vests his brother had in a storage closet. He handed one to Kelly, and he put another on while he went to the front of the house to talk to Cameron. He also grabbed a pair of night-vision goggles. Maybe one of the hands could use them to pinpoint the location of the kidnappers before Kelly and he even reached the old house.

"I want Edwin and you to stay here," Jameson told Cameron. "Gabriel will be here any minute, but we can't wait. When he gets here, just fill him in on what's happening."

"What if he wants to go after you and Kelly?" Cameron asked.

"Then tell him to be careful and let him know about the explosives. Also, make sure everything is still locked up and rearm the security system when we leave." Jameson rattled off the code for him to do that. "And keep watch. I don't want any of those thugs trying to sneak in."

"Please keep our baby safe," Kelly added.

"I'll protect her with my life," Cameron assured her.

Jameson hoped it didn't come down to that. Maybe he could defuse this dangerous situation without Gracelyn being in harm's way.

"Stay behind me," Jameson told Kelly the moment they stepped onto the porch. "And once we're on the trail, I want you to crouch down and use the shrubs and trees for cover."

"But you'll be out in the open," she pointed out.

"They don't want to kill me. They're after you." Not that she needed the reminder. He certainly didn't, either. Because each step they took could be their last.

There were two hands at the front of the house, two more at the back and one on each side. The one on the left side of the steps was Allen Colley, and he had both a sidearm and a rifle.

"Move onto the porch," Jameson told him. "If you see a gunman coming after Kelly and me, try to take him out."

Without hesitation, Allen nodded and did as Jameson said. It wasn't much backup, but it was better than nothing. Plus, maybe there were other hands already in position who could help out if things went from bad to worse.

He also passed Allen the goggles and told the hand to text him if he was able to figure out where the kidnappers were.

Jameson started for the path, and he made sure Kelly was squarely behind him. She was. He also spotted another ranch hand behind a tree just off the trail. Good. Maybe there were others scattered around the grounds.

As soon as they reached the area where the shrubs butted right up against the trail, Kelly ducked lower and went into them. Along with the Kevlar vest, it might protect her. Or at least make her a less visible target.

Jameson had walked this path many times because as a kid, it was the way he got between home and his grandparents' house, where Gabriel was now living. In those days, it had been a pleasant walk with the promise of ice cream or some other treat waiting for him. Definitely nothing pleasant about tonight, though.

"Once we get closer to the house, I want you to get all the way on the ground," Jameson told her. "I'll try one last time to negotiate with the men." But he wasn't holding out much hope for that.

His phone buzzed, and Jameson saw the now-familiar Unknown Caller on the screen.

"Time's up," the man growled when Jameson answered.

That was the only warning Kelly and he got before the shot blasted through the air.

Chapter Sixteen

Kelly wanted to scream for the kidnappers to quit shooting. But her breath froze in her throat. The fear came, too, not just for Boyer's baby but for Gracelyn. Because any shot fired could make it through the walls of Gabriel's house.

Jameson cursed into the phone. "We're coming to you," he snarled to the kidnapper. "But if that baby gets hurt, you've lost your bargaining power with Kelly, and you know it."

"The kid ain't hurt," the man answered. He still sounded arrogant and smug despite the fact that Kelly could also hear the baby crying in the background. "We just wanted to give you some incentive to go faster than you're going now. I'll pull the trigger again in one minute."

Oh, God. That got Kelly moving again. Jameson, too, but he kept the phone right next to them so she'd be able to hear.

"We were going slow because you said there were explosives," Jameson pointed out to the man. "If Kelly is blown up, you'll never get that file. Or whatever it is you want from her."

"The explosives aren't on the path between the two houses. Stay on it, and you'll be fine."

"Right." Jameson made a sound of skepticism. "And I'm to believe you? You just fired a shot with a baby in the room."

"Cowboy, you got no choice but to believe me," the man snapped, and he ended the call.

"Should you text Cameron so he can tell the hands there are no explosives on the path?" she asked. They definitely picked up the pace, but it was a pace and position that put them right out in the open.

Jameson shook his head. "He could have said that to lure them onto the path so he could kill them. Or there really could be explosives here."

That sent her pulse up a notch, something that Kelly hadn't thought possible. It already felt as if her heart were about to beat out of her chest. But what Jameson said was true. There could indeed be explosives, ones that the kidnappers could set off at any time. That thought didn't steady her any.

They continued to walk, probably not hurrying as much as the kidnapper would want, but Jameson and she were trying to keep watch. Not just at the ground but also their surroundings to make sure they weren't about to be ambushed.

Jameson's phone buzzed, and Kelly braced herself for another taunting call from the kidnapper, but it was the ranch hand, Allen. Jameson hit the answer button but then handed it to her. No doubt so it would keep his hands free since there were now very close to the house. As Jameson had done, Kelly held out the phone so they could both hear.

"I used the goggles," Allen said, "and I spotted someone in the side window of the second floor. It's the room at the front of the house. He's got a rifle."

Of course, Kelly had figured the guy would have a weapon like that, but hearing it gave her a new surge of adrenaline. And fear.

"Then there are probably at least two of them," Jameson answered. "Because the photo of the baby was taken downstairs in the family room."

True. The kidnapper could have moved her upstairs, but Kelly doubted he'd do that. It was more likely that he had a comrade or two.

"There are hands in the bushes just off the path," Allen went on, "but I told them to stay put for now."

"Good," Jameson answered. "Are they in position to return fire if it comes down to it?"

"Some should be," Allen assured him. "I got a glimpse of somebody else, too. It's not one of ours. Someone's in a cluster of oak trees in the backyard at the old house. From where you are, you might be able to see him or her."

Both Jameson and she immediately looked in that direction. Nothing. Not at first anyway. Then Kelly caught a blur of motion. A person moving to the back side of the house.

Mandy.

Her sister was right there, and she probably didn't know about the explosives. Well, Mandy didn't unless she'd been the one to hire these snakes who'd put them there.

"I need to try to text or call her so I can warn her," Kelly insisted. Because if her sister was truly innocent, she didn't want her killed. Nor did she want Mandy accidentally setting off a bomb that could hurt the baby.

"Let us know if you see anyone else," Jameson told the hand. "Go ahead and try Mandy," he added right after Kelly had hit the end call button.

Kelly cursed her fingers because they were shaking. Actually, all of her was shaking, but she finally texted the number that Mandy had used to call them earlier. She prayed her sister still had that particular phone with her.

Explosives might be near the house, Kelly texted.

Jameson and she kept walking, her heart

pounding harder with each step. It pounded even harder when she got an answer to the text.

Haven't seen any explosives, Mandy responded. Going into the house now. Try to cover me if you can.

Jameson groaned when Kelly showed him the text. "Tell her to wait until we're there."

Kelly fired off that message but got no response. Worse, Mandy disappeared from sight. Kelly was about to send another text, but the phone buzzed. This time, it was Unknown Caller on the screen, and she immediately hit the answer button.

"We'll be there in under a minute," Jameson assured the caller.

"That's good to hear, but what I want to know is who's in the car that just pulled up on the road in front of the house."

Jameson craned his neck in that direction and shook his head. "I can't see the road. But it's not the cops, if that's what you're thinking."

"Oh, I know it's not them. Well, not your brother anyway. I see the sheriff just pulled up in front of his home sweet home. He used the back road and not the one that runs in front of your folks' place."

That gave Kelly a little relief. Now that Gabriel was there, that was one extra person to protect Gracelyn and the others. Of course,

Gabriel would likely try to help Jameson and her, too.

"When you get into the front yard," the kidnapper continued, "leave Kelly by the porch, and you go to whoever's in that car and tell them to take a hike."

"You're sure it's not one of your fellow hired thugs?" Jameson asked him.

"Nope. I'm thinking this thug is one of yours. Just take care of the problem, or I'll have no use for you, cowboy."

It sickened Kelly to hear that, especially those final words before the kidnapper hung up. To know that no matter what Jameson did, the goons inside would try to kill him anyway. Plus, going up to that car could be just as dangerous as facing whoever was inside the house.

Jameson put his phone away as they reached the edge of the yard. There were still plenty of weeds and underbrush here, too, but they finally had a line of sight of the road.

And Kelly had no trouble seeing the black car.

The driver had stopped beside some thick trees. He'd probably done that with the hope the kidnappers wouldn't be able to spot him since it wasn't visible from the house itself. The fact that the thugs knew the car was there told her that they had some kind of surveillance—either equipment or men—on the road.

"You think it's Boyer?" she whispered.

"Maybe. Or it could be someone Mandy brought with her."

Yes, her sister hadn't said she was alone, but Kelly hadn't seen anyone with Mandy before she'd ducked out of sight.

"Go to the car, cowboy!" someone shouted. It was one of the kidnappers, and he was in the upstairs window. The window was open a fraction, just enough for Kelly to see the barrel of the rifle sticking out. But the man carrying that rifle had stayed in the shadows.

Jameson glanced around as if trying to figure out what to do. The kidnapper had told him to leave her in the yard, but if he did that, they might just try to grab her. However, if Jameson took her with him to the car, the baby's captors might start shooting. But that mental debate came to a quick halt when they heard another shout.

Mandy this time.

"Watch out!" she yelled.

But there wasn't time for Kelly to try to figure out why her sister had given them that warning. That's because the black car on the road exploded into a fireball.

JAMESON AUTOMATICALLY PULLED Kelly to the ground and covered her with his body. Not a second too soon, either. That's because the flaming pieces of the car started raining down on the yard and smacking into the house. He heard glass shattering and something else.

The baby crying.

Hell. Jameson prayed that she hadn't been hurt and was just frightened from the noise.

"Mandy," Kelly said, her voice as ragged as her breathing. "She called out right before the explosion."

"I don't think she was near the car."

Jameson hadn't been able to pinpoint her voice, but he thought it might have come from the other side of the house. That's where the family room was located. And the baby if they hadn't moved her. If Mandy was indeed there, the line of trees should have protected the debris from getting to her.

"You would have been killed if you'd gone closer," Kelly said, her voice as ragged as her breathing.

Yeah. In fact, they still could have been killed if one of those metal chunks had hit them. There were huge pieces of what was left of the car scattered all around them. The question now was—had there been anyone in that car? If so, they were dead.

"Why would the kidnappers do this?" Kelly asked. "Why would they take a risk like that?"

"I'm not sure they did," Jameson mumbled.

From that second-floor window, the kidnapper was cursing. Clearly, he wasn't pleased with what had just happened, which meant either it was malfunctioning explosives or someone else had set it off.

Someone, maybe, like Boyer?

But that didn't feel right, either. Boyer seemed to love his little girl, and he wouldn't want to put her at risk. Of course, it was possible that Boyer had just gotten unlucky and parked on one of the explosive devices the thugs had set.

Jameson's phone dinged with a text message, but he passed it to Kelly because he didn't want to take his eyes off their surroundings.

"It's Gabriel," she relayed. "He's on the way down here."

Not exactly the best news, but Jameson doubted he could stop his big brother. "Tell him to watch for explosives."

While she was doing that, Jameson saw some movement on the far side of the house. Mandy. She was leaning out and looking in their direction. Kelly saw her, too, because she lifted her head, tracking her sister as Mandy moved to the front porch. Jameson wanted to throttle her for that. It was too big of a risk, and if she wasn't the one behind this, she was going to get herself killed.

"Cowboy," the kidnapper shouted. "You and Kelly can start moving again now."

"Is the baby okay?" Jameson demanded.

"For now. Keep it that way, and do as I say. You walk to the center of the front yard. Better find a spot that's not on fire from your little prank. I'm guessing that was your brother's doing."

Not a chance. But Jameson kept that to himself. "What about Kelly?"

"I want her on the front porch. And no more lollygagging around. Move fast."

Kelly started to stand up, but Jameson pulled her back down. "I can't stop this," he said, and that ate away at him. He could lose her, right here, right now. "But let me go out there first. That way, I can be in position to pick off anyone who tries to shoot. And when you get to the porch, drop down by the steps. They're stone, and they'll give you some cover."

She nodded, staring at him, and even in the moonlight, he could see the fear in her eyes. "What about you?"

"I'll take cover, too." Though he wasn't exactly sure where that would be yet. Nor did he have time to work it out now. Jameson just had to pray that the kidnappers didn't gun them down the moment they stepped into the yard.

"I love you," she said, dropping a kiss on his mouth.

It wasn't a good time to be stunned, but that's exactly what those words did to Jameson. They probably weren't even true. This could just be Kelly's way of saying goodbye. Well, it wasn't goodbye for him. One way or another, he was going to save her and get them out of this.

"Move it now!" the kidnapper shouted. "And remember, no guns."

Jameson did. He got up, tucking his gun in the back waist of his jeans. He walked out into the yard. Fast. He fired glances all around them, especially at the house and Kelly. But he saw Mandy, too. She was crawling her way to the door. He shook his head, but Jameson doubted it would do any good.

Behind him, he heard a strange sound. A gasp. And he whirled around in that direction to see something he damn sure didn't want to see.

Kelly.

She was on her feet, but she wasn't alone. There was a man behind her, and he had a gun. Jameson got just a glimpse of him before the guy fired a shot. Not at Kelly. But at Jameson.

It slammed into his chest.

He heard Kelly scream. There was nothing he could do about it, though. The pain exploded inside him, and Jameson had no choice but to drop to his knees. The bullet had hit the Kevlar, but it had knocked the breath out of him. Had maybe cracked some ribs, too, and the hot metal was burning a hole in him. But the worst part was, he couldn't get to Kelly.

And the man who'd shot him had now put the gun to Kelly's head.

Jameson got a better look at him then. Saw the man whispering something in Kelly's ear.

That man was August Canton.

KELLY TRIED TO call out to Jameson, but her throat had clamped shut. Oh, God. He'd been shot. And it didn't matter that she couldn't see any blood. He was down on the ground, writhing in pain and clutching his chest. He needed help.

Help that she couldn't give him because the man had her in a choke hold.

Too bad she couldn't use her gun; her captor had stripped that from her the moment he'd grabbed her.

That didn't stop her from fighting, though. She tried to slam her elbow into his stomach so she could break free from him, but she failed.

He dodged her blow, tightened his grip on her and dug the barrel of his gun against her temple.

"Move and I shoot Jameson again," he growled right in her ear. "And this time, the bullet goes in his head."

As sickening as that threat was, what twisted at her even more was that she recognized that voice. She hadn't managed to see the man before he'd grabbed her, but she knew who their attacker was now. August.

"Why?" she managed to ask. However, Kelly already knew the answer. This had to do with that blasted file.

A file that no doubt incriminated August in some way. Or so he thought. But Kelly honestly didn't remember if there was anything in there that would do that.

"Now, let's go into the house and wait for Gabriel." August started pushing her in that direction. "Then we can really settle some things."

"What about Jameson?" The grip he had on her throat made it hard for her to speak. Hard to breathe, too.

"Oh, he'll be coming, too. This plan wouldn't be complete without him."

That sounded like the vile threat that it was, and she prayed Jameson would be able to move soon so he could scramble out of the way.

Kelly looked on the porch but didn't see her sister. Maybe that meant Mandy had slipped inside. Of course, that didn't mean Mandy was in there to help them out. No. She could be working for August and these thugs. Or for Boyer.

But where was the agent?

And where was Gabriel? She still had Jameson's phone, but there hadn't been a text message. It was possible, though, that Gabriel had already seen what was going on and was trying to figure out a way to stop it.

"This would be a bad time for cops to arrive," August warned her. "Anyone who comes near the house now will die."

She figured that applied to anyone who went inside the house, too, and that's exactly where August was taking her.

"I don't remember where the file is," she lied. She couldn't offer to give it to him, because once he had it, she had no bargaining power whatsoever.

"Then I'll torture Jameson and Gabriel until you do remember."

August kept dragging her across the yard, and when she got closer to Jameson, he looked at her. She could see the pain etched on his face, and he was fighting to get the vest off him. Probably because the bullet was burning like fire.

"If you try to get up, I'll shoot Kelly," August snarled to Jameson, and he kept on moving up the steps and onto the porch. When they went inside the house, though, August froze. "Randy," he called out.

There was some movement in the adjacent room, but apparently something was wrong. She could tell by the way August's arm tensed. Maybe the hired thug was supposed to swoop out and get her so that his boss could deal with Jameson.

Finally, a man staggered into the foyer. There was blood streaming down his face, and he was mumbling profanity. "That bitch sister of hers clubbed me on the head, grabbed the baby and climbed out the window with her."

Despite everything else that was going on, that caused relief to flood through Kelly. Mandy had gotten the child, and maybe her sister would be able to get the little girl safely away from all of this. It also meant that Mandy wasn't working for August.

"Have someone find her now," August growled. "She could have seen me."

That told Kelly plenty about this situation. August didn't intend on leaving any witnesses behind because he planned on getting away with this. And she soon saw how he'd intended to do that.

Someone had used what appeared to be red paint or maybe blood to write on the foyer walls.

Time for more Becketts to die.

Back to finish what I started ten years ago.

August was going to make it look as if the "real" killer had returned to the scene of the crime. And she doubted the timing was a coincidence, since it was the decade anniversary of the murders.

"You killed them," she said. "You murdered Jameson's parents."

August certainly didn't deny it. He turned her so that she was facing the door. That meant if anyone came charging in through there, he would use her as a human shield.

"Have someone bring in Jameson," August ordered his thug. The guy was still bleeding, still looked pretty shaky, but he was repeating August's order through a small communicator.

"That's why you want my file," Kelly pressed. Along with the fear, the anger roared through her. "You butchered two people, and you've let your brother rot in jail this whole time."

August cursed her and whacked his gun against the side of her head. It hurt—bad, but she'd obviously hit a nerve.

"My brother will be released once the law finds this new crime scene," August insisted.

"No. He won't be. Unless there's proof someone else did the killings. Planted proof..." She stopped, groaned. "You're going to set up Boyer. That's why you took his child, so that he would come out here. Where is he? Do you have him tied up somewhere?"

"He was in the car that exploded. Don't worry. There's enough evidence on his computer to convince the cops he did this."

A hoarse sob tore from her mouth. She certainly hadn't cared much for Boyer, but if August was telling the truth, then he'd just made Amy an orphan. Worse, August planned to get away with all of this death, pain and misery.

But Kelly didn't intend to let that happen.

Somehow, she had to stop him.

There was some movement by the front door, and Kelly steeled herself up for more thugs. However, it was Jameson. He still had that pained look on his face, was still having trouble moving, but one of the hired guns shoved him into the foyer, sending Jameson to the floor.

Without thinking, Kelly tried to break free and go to him. And she paid for that when August hit her with the gun again. The pain was the least of what she felt, though. She saw the rage that put in Jameson's eyes, and he came off the floor, ready to launch himself at August.

"Don't," August warned him, "because I'll kill her where she stands."

"I got his guns," the thug informed his boss. "And the sheriff is here. He's in those bushes off the trail where you were waiting."

August's arm muscles relaxed a little. "Good. Bring him here so I can finish this."

If looks could have killed, Jameson's glare would have blasted August to smithereens. "Why?" Jameson growled, his voice low and dangerous.

"Because I have to do something to get Travis out of jail. And that file that Kelly and you put together has too many pieces that can lead back to me. I'd hoped that you two wouldn't find so much, but I knew if you did that you'd be easier to take care of than the cops."

"What pieces?" Kelly asked. "Because I'd like to know the reason I'm about to die."

"It's the interviews with Hattie's friends," August said after a long pause. "Not the official ones. But the later ones that Jameson did. He talked to them, the other folks in the area."

She had to shake her head. "Hattie, the woman you milked out of her savings? The woman who died?"

"The woman who started Sheriff Sherman

Beckett's investigation into me. Sherman was a little too good at his job, because he started poking around in other things I was involved in. Like money laundering."

"And that's why you murdered him," Kelly concluded. "I'm guessing, though, that his wife was just collateral damage. She probably walked in while you were killing her husband, and she tried to stop it."

August didn't deny any of that.

"This is all for nothing," Kelly assured him. "Because there wasn't anything in those secondary interviews to incriminate you."

"Yes, there was. If you dig hard, you'll see there's a problem with my alibi. When you talked to Marilyn, she got the times wrong. Stupid woman."

"We have the sheriff," the wounded thug said to August. "They're bringing him in now."

Kelly's stomach went to her knees. She'd hoped that Gabriel might be able to escape. Now this meant August would get all of the key players in the house. Where he would kill them.

"Tell them to hurry getting Gabriel here," August told the goon as he checked his watch. "Time is running out."

What did he have up his sleeve now? She didn't want to wait around and find out.

Her eyes locked with Jameson, and Kelly could sense he was about to do something. What exactly, she didn't know, but she didn't have to wait long to find out.

Jameson lunged forward, and in the same motion, he shoved the hired gun who'd brought him inside. The thug flew right into August and her, and it felt as if a Mack truck had hit her. But she instantly knew why Jameson had done that. That's because they all fell, and she heard at least one of the guns clattering to the floor.

August spewed out some vile profanity, and from the corner of her eye, Kelly saw the bleeding gunman about to join the fray. She put a stop to that by tripping him. He dropped down next to them, and she snatched up his gun.

But she didn't have a shot.

August, Jameson and now both thugs were in a fierce battle, and she couldn't fire for fear of hitting Jameson. Worse, the third gunman was probably about to come in at any moment, and since he had Gabriel, he would be able to stop this by threatening to kill Jameson's brother. That's why Kelly had to do something now.

She shifted the gun in her hand and bashed

it against the wounded man's head. He howled in pain and rolled out of the heap.

And that's when Kelly took aim and shot him. Not to disable him, either. She went for a kill shot, and she made it.

With that one out of the way, she turned back to the fight. Jameson had August pinned to the floor, but her heart skipped a couple of beats when she saw the hired thug lift his gun toward Jameson. Since she couldn't risk firing, she kicked him as hard as she could. His muscles were rock-hard, and it didn't even seem to faze him, but it did cause the goon to look back at her.

Big mistake.

Because Jameson took advantage of that. Even though the man was much larger than he was, Jameson managed to take hold of him, and he shoved him at August.

Just as August fired off a shot.

A shot that went straight into his man.

Even in the darkness, Kelly saw the look of shock on August's face. For a split second anyway, before Jameson grabbed August and dragged him to his feet. Kelly quickly handed Jameson her gun, and he put it to the man's head.

She could feel the rage in Jameson. The need for him to avenge his parents' death. The muscles in his jaw were tight. His hands were shaking a little. And the moments crawled by with his finger tensing on the trigger.

Kelly also saw the exact moment Jameson remembered he was a lawman and not a killer. Nothing like the piece of slime he was holding.

"August Canton, you're under arrest," Jameson gutted out.

Behind her, Kelly heard the footsteps on the porch. This was no doubt Gabriel being led in by one of August's henchmen. She snatched up the dead thug's gun so she could use it to free Gabriel.

But there was no need for that.

Gabriel was alone. And unharmed. He came into the foyer, and he took in the scene with a sweeping glance. His eyes met Jameson's. Even though they didn't say anything, a dozen things passed between them. All the pain and loss. All the grief they'd suffered for the past ten years.

"The ranch hands have rounded up the hired guns," Gabriel said. His voice was a little unsteady, but that was a vicious glare he had nailed to August. "Let's get him locked up."

Gabriel used some plastic cuffs to restrain August, but when Kelly looked at the man, she saw something she didn't like.

August was smiling.

"Always have a backup plan," August taunted. He glanced at his watch again. His smile widened.

Just as the sound of the explosion ripped through the house.

Chapter Seventeen

One second Jameson was standing, and the next he was back on the floor. Somehow, he managed to catch on to Kelly and break her fall, and she landed in his arms. The pain shot through him again because that definitely hadn't helped with the ribs he was certain he'd cracked.

The pain was the least of his worries, though. "Run!" Gabriel shouted. He, too, was on the floor next to August, and his brother hauled the man to his feet and headed for the front door.

Jameson did the same to Kelly. Not easily, but he got her moving. And that's when he realized the entire back half of the house was missing. There was a groaning sound, and the roof came swooshing down, the ceiling and boards clattering all around them.

Thankfully, Kelly seemed to be able to run, so maybe that meant she hadn't been hurt. Except he saw the blood on her forehead. It was possible they hadn't gotten so lucky after all.

With Gabriel gripping August, they ran down the porch steps and into the yard. Not a second too soon. Because the entire house fell right in front of them. Debris went everywhere, mixing with the burning car parts that were still all around them.

"Take my truck," Gabriel said, tossing Jameson the keys. "It's parked on the road just up from here. You and Kelly get back to the house, and Cameron and I will take this piece of scum to jail."

August sure as heck wasn't smiling now. He looked back at what was left of the house, and his nostrils flared. His face twisted into an enraged snarl. As arrogant as he was, the last thing he'd probably expected was to fail.

But he had.

Thank God, he had.

Even though Gabriel had said the hands had rounded up August's goons, Jameson didn't want to risk her being out in the open any longer. He hooked his arm around her waist and got her into Gabriel's truck. The moment he had her inside, he started the engine and got them moving. He also glanced at Kelly to see if that bleeding on her head had gotten any worse.

"It's just a scratch," she said, following his gaze and then touching her fingers to her forehead. "But you need to see a doctor. You wince in pain every time you move."

Yeah, he was wincing, but Jameson had hoped she hadn't noticed. "We'll both see the doctor in an hour or two. Once we're sure the scene has been cleared."

Her eyes widened, and she made a soft moan. "You think those men—"

"No. I just want to make sure all the explosives are gone." With August's sick mind, he could have planted others. Heck, he could have done it weeks or even months ago, since he'd apparently been planning this for years.

Kelly didn't exactly breathe any easier, but he hoped once she saw that Gracelyn was all right, that it would help steady her nerves. Jameson did something that he figured definitely wouldn't calm her, but he couldn't help himself. He kissed her when he pulled to a stop in front of Gabriel's house.

He'd been wrong, though, about it not helping. Because he could feel some of the tension leave her body. It helped him, too, but he definitely didn't want to start a make-out session in the truck. Not with a deputy and his sister-in-law watching from the windows. Jameson got her moving, and they hurried up the steps into the house.

"Thank God, you're all right," Jodi immediately said. She gave them both hugs. "Gabriel?" He saw the worry in her eyes, too.

"He's fine. He arrested August."

"August?" someone repeated. Ivy. His sister was at the top of the stairs.

There was plenty he could tell her, but this wasn't the time for it. Not with their emotions still so raw. "August is the one who killed Mom and Dad."

Ivy shook her head, as if she might not believe that, but then a sob tore from her mouth. He pulled his sister into his arms. A hug wasn't much, but maybe knowing the truth would finally help them all heal.

"Where's Gracelyn?" Kelly asked, taking the question right out of Jameson's mouth.

"Still in the bathroom with Erica. They're both fine," Ivy added. She moved out of Jameson's embrace so he could head up the stairs.

But he came to a quick halt.

That's because there was someone in the family room. Mandy. And she was holding a little girl. Boyer's daughter, no doubt.

"I started running and didn't know where else to go," Mandy said, her voice raw and broken. The baby seemed all right, though. In fact, she was sleeping in Mandy's arms. "Boyer's dead, isn't he?"

Kelly nodded. "August said he was in the car that exploded."

"He was." Tears shimmered in Mandy's eyes. "I saw him, but I figured if I didn't get to the baby, those men could hurt her."

"They could have," Jameson assured her. "You did the right thing getting her out. A dangerous thing," he tacked onto that. But it was hard to argue with something that had worked to save a child.

"I didn't have anything to do with August's plan or the attacks," Mandy insisted, her gaze shifting to her sister. "I love you and want you safe."

"I believe you," Kelly answered. "And I love you, too."

Kelly said the words as easily to Mandy as she had to him right before all hell had broken loose. She sounded sincere. Both now and then. But Jameson wasn't sure if the *I love you* she'd given him was because she had been afraid they were going to die.

"I'll have to go to jail, won't I?" Mandy asked. "Because I'm the one who took Amy. I'm the one who kept her from Boyer. But I swear I thought it was dangerous. I believed what Hadley told me about him."

Jameson would have liked to reassure her that all would be well. He couldn't. After all,

Mandy had committed a felony, and that meant she almost certainly would do some jail time.

"What will happen to Amy if I'm arrested?" Mandy pressed.

Kelly went to her, and as Jodi had done to them, she hugged her sister. She also brushed a kiss on the baby's forehead. "I'll make sure Amy is taken care of while we look for her next of kin."

That was the right thing to say, and Jameson would indeed do just that. Heck, if they couldn't find any of her relatives, he could raise her himself.

That mentally stopped him.

He had obviously jumped right into daddy mode. But there was no way he was going to let Amy go into foster care, not after everything she'd been through.

"Should I, uh, go ahead and arrest Mandy?" Edwin asked.

"Not yet. Let her stay with the baby awhile longer." It was the best Jameson could offer her under the circumstances. "But if Mandy tries to run—"

"I won't," Mandy interrupted. "No way do I want her back out there with possible explosives." She cradled the baby closer and rocked her.

Later, he'd need to have a long chat with

Mandy about all the details of the attacks that she might have witnessed, but it was just routine. Jameson didn't expect any more surprises. At least he hoped like the devil there wouldn't be. He'd had enough surprises to last him a lifetime.

Or so he thought.

But when Kelly and he went into the bathroom, and he saw his daughter, Jameson couldn't believe that he loved someone as much as he loved her. It was incredible and terrifying at the same time. And somehow perfect.

Gracelyn was asleep in Erica's arms, but the baby opened her eyes and turned her head toward them. She gave them a sleepy smile before closing her eyes. Oh, man. There it was again. That punch of emotion. He went to her and eased Gracelyn from Erica.

"Is everything okay?" Erica whispered.

"It is now." Jameson brushed a kiss on Gracelyn's cheek and handed her to Kelly so she could do the same.

Erica made a sound of relief, and she must have sensed they needed some alone time because she excused herself and left.

Kelly gave the baby another kiss and looked up at him. There was still blood on her face, and he grabbed a tissue to wipe it away. The nicks and bruises were reminders of the hell they'd just gone through. But they would heal. In a week or so, there'd be no signs of all the bad stuff.

Plus, there was good, too.

Kelly smiled at him, and it gave him that same flood of warmth as Gracelyn's smile. She kept staring at him. Maybe waiting for him to say something. He had plenty to say all right, but he didn't even get a chance to start because his phone buzzed. Jameson answered it right away when he saw Gabriel's name on the screen.

"Please tell me August didn't escape," Jameson said. He walked into the adjacent bedroom so the conversation wouldn't wake up Gracelyn, but when Kelly followed him, he put the call on speaker.

"No. We just arrived at the station, and he's behind bars."

Jameson released the breath he'd been holding. August had evaded justice for a decade, and he didn't want the man getting away with anything else. "Has he said anything?"

"Yeah. Mostly curse words I won't repeat. He blames me and you for not finding someone other than Travis to convict for the murders."

That was warped logic, but then, August was a warped man. "If August was so torn up about his brother being behind bars, why didn't he just confess to the crime he committed?"

"I asked him that, and he put the blame on Dad for investigating him."

Yeah, August was definitely too far gone to see that he was the monster in all of this. And his arrogance and stupidity had caused a lot of pain and misery.

"In one of August's profanity tirades," Gabriel continued, "he did let it slip that he's the one who's been sending us threats."

Well, that was one thing cleared up. But once August had revealed himself as the killer, Jameson had just assumed he'd made the threats, too. And August had probably done that to try to make them think that either there was a copycat or they'd put the wrong man in jail.

Which they had.

"All the evidence pointed to Travis," Gabriel said as if reading his mind. "Since August insists he didn't set him up, I suspect Travis went by the house shortly after the murders, and that's how he got Dad's blood on his shirt."

That was possible, since Travis was their neighbor. Plus, the man had been drunk, so he wouldn't have even realized how incriminating it would have been to touch the body.

Jameson looked at Kelly to see how she was dealing with all of this. Her forehead was bunched up, and there was concern in her eyes. But he thought the worry was for him. For how he was handling all this discussion about his parents. He went to her and kissed her to let her know he was okay.

And he was.

His folks' deaths would always cut him to the bone, but there were new things in his life to help with the hurt. Mainly Kelly and Gracelyn.

"We'll go through everything that's in Kelly's file," Gabriel continued a moment later. "And I'll contact the warden of the prison to let him know that Travis will soon be getting out."

It wouldn't be easy, but Jameson planned to be there for the man's release. He wanted to look Travis in the eyes and tell him he was sorry for the conviction. After all, Travis's son and daughter were now part of the Beckett family, and Jameson wanted a fresh start for all of them. Well, everyone except August. The man would almost certainly end up on death row.

"Any idea who August planned to set up to take the fall for the murders?" Jameson asked his brother.

"I think Boyer."

Jameson made a sound of agreement. "When we were in the house, August mentioned putting something on Boyer's computer that would incriminate him." And now Boyer was dead. "Boyer's baby is here at your place," Jameson added.

"Edwin called and told me. After the CSI team and reserve deputies are in place, I'll have Edwin bring in Mandy. I can't make the charges against her go away, though."

"I know," Kelly said. "My sister has to pay for what she's done." She paused. "But maybe the baby can stay here and not be sent to foster care?"

"I'm pretty sure I can arrange that." Now it was Gabriel's turn to hesitate. "Are you two sure, though, that you can manage a second baby? I mean, you're going to be settling in with Gracelyn."

Settling in. That was an interesting choice of words. Was that what Kelly and he were doing?

"We can do this," Kelly assured his brother. "Well, with some help from the rest of you."

"Are we talking changing diapers?" Gabriel asked. There was a touch of humor in his voice.

"Definitely," Jameson answered. And he found himself smiling. Gabriel was going to be a good uncle, and one day a good father.

"All right," Gabriel agreed. "I'll change a diaper or two. Will even babysit some. What I want to know, though, is how soon will Kelly and Gracelyn be moving in with you?"

Good question, but Jameson didn't have the

answer. "I'll get back to you on that. Let me know if anything else comes up."

"And you let me know when Kelly and you set a wedding date." Chuckling, Gabriel ended the call.

Jameson scowled at the phone and would give his brother a scowl in person later. Gabriel's comment had no doubt shocked Kelly. It was too soon for her to even be thinking about long-term plans...

Or not.

She slid her hand around the back of his neck, eased him closer and kissed him. Really kissed him. In fact, it was as hot and close as it could be considering that she was still holding Gracelyn. When she'd rid him of every trace of the scowl and made him pretty much mindless, she pulled back.

Smiled.

"I'm in love with you," she said. "That wasn't the fear or the adrenaline talking. I meant it. I fell in love with you two years ago, and the feelings are still as strong as ever."

Good. That was exactly what he wanted to hear.

Jameson pulled Kelly back into his arms and gave the words right back to her. "I'm in love with you, too."

He kissed her mouth. That smile. And then kissed her again.

Everything he'd ever wanted was right here in his arms—his precious little girl and the woman he loved.

* * * * *

Get 2 Free Books,
Plus 2 Free Gifts—
just for trying the Reader Service!

HARLEQUIN
ROMANTIC suspense

Get 2 Free Books,
Plus 2 Free Gifts—

just for trying the
Reader Service!

HARLEQUIN *Presents*